SUCH A GOOD GIRL

ALSO BY AMANDA K. MORGAN

Secrets, Lies, and Scandals

SUCH A GOOD GIRL

AMANDA K. MORGAN

Simon Pulse

New York   London   Toronto   Sydney   New Delhi

This book is a work of fiction. Any references to historical events, real people, or real places are used fictitiously. Other names, characters, places, and events are products of the author's imagination, and any resemblance to actual events or places or persons, living or dead, is entirely coincidental.

Simon Pulse

An imprint of Simon & Schuster Children's Publishing Division
1230 Avenue of the Americas, New York, New York 10020
First Simon Pulse hardcover edition June 2017
Text copyright © 2017 by Simon & Schuster, Inc.
Front and spine jacket photograph copyright © 2017 by Arcangel/Vicky Martin
Jacket flaps photograph of ribbon copyright © 2017 by Thinkstock
Front case illustration copyright © 2017 by Thinkstock
All rights reserved, including the right of reproduction in whole or in part in any form.
SIMON PULSE and colophon are registered trademarks of Simon & Schuster, Inc.
For information about special discounts for bulk purchases, please contact Simon & Schuster Special Sales at 1-866-506-1949 or business@simonandschuster.com.
The Simon & Schuster Speakers Bureau can bring authors to your live event.
For more information or to book an event contact the Simon & Schuster Speakers Bureau at 1-866-248-3049 or visit our website at www.simonspeakers.com.
Jacket designed by Jessica Handelman
Interior designed by Mike Rosamilia
The text of this book was set in ITC New Baskerville.
Manufactured in the United States of America
2 4 6 8 10 9 7 5 3 1
This book has been cataloged with the Library of Congress.
ISBN 978-1-4814-4957-1 (hc)
ISBN 978-1-4814-4959-5 (eBook)

For Ryan and Lindsay

Something to Know About Riley Stone:

- Riley Elizabeth Stone is just about perfect. Ask anyone.

ONE
Perfect

"What was it like being the homecoming queen as a freshman?"

Sydnee Grace Hill, a first-semester reporter for the high school newspaper, smiles across from me at a cramped table at Hartsville High's answer for a school café. She's writing a student profile on me for the next issue. Each month, a senior is chosen. They asked me back in August, but I was really busy with a fund-raiser for a local no-kill animal shelter, so they scooted me back a few issues.

"Oh." I smile at the reporter, a little impressed. She's done her homework. Well, she's tried, at least. "I wasn't exactly the homecoming queen, Syd."

Sydnee, a freshman herself, blushes at the nickname. "Yeah, but you got the most votes, didn't you?"

"Sure, but votes didn't matter. Freshmen didn't qualify. I think Madison Corrigan ended up getting it that year," I say, like I don't remember the exact moment they told me that I wouldn't be crowned homecoming queen and announced Maddie instead, a cold-hearted senior with white-blond hair who was known for publicly embarrassing freshmen in front of her senior posse. She made them hold her books outside the restroom and do her laundry (including panties and sweaty gym clothes) and even forced them to do her homework, like that was supposed to somehow increase their social standing.

It was definitely a travesty.

"You won this year, though," Sydnee points out. "And you've made homecoming court every single year."

I nod, smiling a little. It's humbling, knowing everyone likes you that much, and that you haven't intimidated your way into it. And scary. "It's an honor," I tell her, and I mean it. I really do.

She writes down my words verbatim. Her big red curls fall in her face and a couple of strands stick to her bubblegum-pink lip gloss.

"Can I fact-check a couple of things for the profile?" she asks. "Just to make sure I get everything right? I mean, if you have time?" Her voice wobbles.

I nod. "Sure."

"You've been accepted to Yale, Stanford, and Harvard, correct?"

"Almost. Not Harvard. Brown, actually."

I watch as she ticks off the names of the correct colleges and

SUCH A GOOD GIRL

scratches out Harvard. She clears her throat. "Right. And you've been captain of the cheerleading squad for . . . ?"

"Two years now. Ever since Ilana Giavanni tore her ACL."

Sydnee nods and scribbles another note. I want to ask her to use her phone to record so the interview will move more quickly, but she seems so nervous I don't want to make it worse. This is probably her first ever interview for the *Harts High Beat* (and yes, that *is* the worst name for a newspaper ever) and I don't want her to think she's doing a bad job. She's actually doing pretty well. I once was interviewed by this boy who couldn't even write because his hands were shaking so hard. Poor thing.

"And you've had a 4.0—since forever?"

I laugh. "I think I got a lackluster grade in handwriting once. But yeah, my grades have been pretty good since—just say high school, okay?"

Sydnee's brow furrows. "Okay. Now, the fun stuff. Eye color, blue . . . height . . . five seven . . . hair color . . . blond?"

I fluff my hair. "Um, my hairstylist makes it look natural, doesn't he?" I laugh. "I'm kind of a dirty blond. Or a lackluster brunette."

She covers her mouth, like I told her some kind of dirty secret. "Am I allowed to publish that? That you're not a real blonde?"

"You can publish where I get it done, for all I care. Maybe he'll give me a discount for the free ad space." I laugh again, and Sydnee giggles, high-pitched and eager.

"Is Hartsville your hometown?" she asks.

"Born and raised."

"Okay. Now I need an embarrassing story."

"Hmm." I tap my lips. "I once got trapped in an elevator."

Sydnee's eyes widen. "What? How is that embarrassing? That sounds horrifying!"

"Well, it was. Except that I had just downed, like, an entire grande caramel brulée latte before getting on the elevator, and I was in there, alone, for almost four hours."

Syndee's eyes go super wide and round. "So what happened? Did you pee your pants?"

"Um, remember the empty Starbucks cup?"

"You didn't."

I nod, and Sydnee covers her mouth.

"By the time I got rescued, I had a full coffee cup with me. I just pretended it was, like, leftover latte, but you could totally smell it. It was pretty gross. The guy who rescued me actually made a face."

Sydnee chokes and then clears her throat. "Are you—are you sure you actually want this to be published in the paper, Riley?"

I laugh. "I don't care. It's funny, right?"

She nods. "Um, yeah. It's just crazy."

"You can't take everything so seriously, Sydnee."

Sydnee lifts a shoulder to her ear.

I stand up from the table. "I have to meet my family for dinner, but if you have any more questions, you can text me, okay?"

She blinks at me. "On your phone? I mean—you—are you sure?"

I smile. "Yeah, sure. Just let me know, okay?"

Sydnee unlocks her phone and hands it to me, and I enter my number as RILEY STONE !☺! 👄. I try to hand it back to

SUCH A GOOD GIRL

her, but she's just staring at me, all trembly and owl-eyed, like I'm sort of celebrity, so I swoop in and give her a hug and a pat on the shoulder and then I just leave her phone on her notepad.

"Don't hesitate to text or whatever, okay, Syd?" I put my sunglasses on, sweep my (dyed) blond hair over my shoulder, and leave the freshman alone at the school café. "I can't wait to see it in the paper. You'll let me know when it runs, won't you?"

"Next . . . next week. See you later, okay, Riley Stone?"

"See you, Sydnee." I smile big at her, trying to communicate that we're cool, and she's cool, and maybe she doesn't have to be so scared next time.

"This came for you," Mom says, handing me a neat white envelope with *Princeton University* emblazoned on the corner. We're all standing around in the kitchen, like we always do, but Dad's the only one really cooking. Mom's just getting things out of the refrigerator for him, setting them close by in case he needs them, like she's actually part of the process or something. She's pretty awful at it—cooking, baking, you name it. She can barely slap together a peanut butter sandwich without causing some serious damage. Dad has the talent, and right now he's stirring his signature red sauce while it simmers on the stove top, filling the kitchen with a warm, rich, garlicky scent that would put most Italian restaurants to shame.

"Do you want to try it?" my dad asks absently, not really expecting anyone to take him up on it. He knows it's good already. It's always good.

7

AMANDA K. MORGAN

"Um, Mom, did you see what's on this envelope?" I wave it at her. Princeton. I didn't get accepted early decision there, but I don't really see any reason why I wouldn't have been. I know what's inside but I want her to just look at me, just for a second. "Mom."

I ease my finger under the envelope.

"Just a minute, honey." She's turned away and already talking to Ethan, my brother, and smiling down on him with her hands on her svelte hips. He's gotten into the garlic bread and has crumbs in the scraggly beard he's trying to grow. He brushes at them with the back of his hand, and they fall into his lap.

"How is she?" my mom is asking in a low voice, like the whole family doesn't already know that his girlfriend is six months knocked up.

With another man's child.

So scandalous.

I tear off a piece of the garlic bread for myself. "Yeah, how is she?" I ask, not because I'm being nasty or anything . . . but because I really want to know. His girlfriend's name is Esther and she's Mother Teresa, except six months pregnant, because she fell in love with the wrong guy, which was Not Ethan, before she fell in love with the right guy, which is Hopefully Ethan.

"She's good," Ethan says. "I'm going with her to her next doctor's appointment."

Mom glows at him. "That's sweet of you, honey."

I feel a little twinge beneath my breastbone. Here I am, getting greasy garlic-bread hands all over my letter from Princeton, and Mom doesn't really care. But get my brother to go to his pregnant

8

SUCH A GOOD GIRL

girlfriend's doctor's appointment, and she's practically a living, breathing parental seal of approval.

I bite back my disappointment. Maybe all I need for some attention is something growing in utero.

I sit down at the kitchen table across from my brother while Dad takes the sauce off the stove and pours it into a white serving bowl. I stuff the garlic bread in my mouth all at once—Sydnee and everyone at school would *so* disapprove—and open my Princeton letter.

"Dear Riley E. Stone," I say through the mouthful of bread. I take a big drink of water and swallow it down. "We are pleased to inform you that you have been accepted into Princeton University's 2022 freshman class."

Dad turns toward me and favors me with a smile. "That's great, sweetie." He turns back to his spaghetti, takes it off the burner, and begins to drain the noodles. The hot water hisses as it hits the stainless steel of the sink.

Mom pats me on the shoulder sort of halfheartedly and Ethan fist-bumps me.

"Is Esther coming over for dinner, Ethan darling?" Mom asks my brother.

"She can invite her family," Dad says from the stove. "I've made plenty. Can you ask them to pick up wine, though, if her parents do come? I think a nice red could go well with this, but I haven't bought any in ages."

"Probably not. Her dad's on a business trip," Ethan says. "Dunno about her mom and sisters." He gives me a little smile. I

9

think he feels bad. He's always stealing my thunder a little bit, without even meaning to. He's just that sort of person. Magnetic. Even when he's doing something utterly without merit.

He's the type of man who could lead an entire army into a meaningless battle and they'd fight with fervor.

In fact, in high school, he got suspended for two weeks when his Spanish teacher realized he was cutting class to host a twenty-man Call of Duty tournament (pay to play with a cash prize) in the school auditorium, and even after ten of the twenty players joined him (in less-serious punishments, obviously, as Ethan was found to be the ringleader) he still made out with, like, a thousand dollars. And then he just moved the tournaments to our basement when our parents weren't home.

My father sets the noodles in the middle of the table and follows it with the bowl of rich sauce, steaming from the stove. "I hear Purdue is really great," he tells me. "You're very lucky to be accepted."

I look down at the Princeton letter. I've left buttery yellow smudges all over it.

"Purdue is really great," I repeat.

No one bothers to correct my father, but I'm not entirely sure they know he was wrong to start with. They start passing around the noodles. Mom wants Parmesan cheese, so I run to the refrigerator and grate a little into a tiny red bowl.

"Food's perfect, Dad," I tell him.

TWO
Posse

There is nothing better in high school than being assigned to your own private study hall room with your two very best friends.

Of course, that's a bit of an exaggeration. I'm sure there are some better things.

For example, all-expenses-paid trips to Europe, or winning a brand-new Lexus with, like, heated and cooled seats and Wi-Fi, or an utterly perfect fake ID. But all of those seem far-fetched because (a) my mom swears that international travel is unsafe right now, (b) my dad says that my car is perfectly acceptable, thank you very much, and (c) honestly, I'm way too much of a rule-follower to purchase a fake ID, let alone *use* one.

I am a girl who takes acceptable risks.

However, as far as reasonably cool stuff, a private study hall isn't terrible or anything. Two years ago, the school got some sort of major grant and completely redid our library—which meant these little pods they added where students can study in a more private, soundproof environment where they're free to listen to music while they work (at an acceptable volume, of course) or collaborate in study groups. Best of all, the pods have actual doors, which means that for one hour, every other day, Kolbie, Neta, and I get (some) privacy to basically hang out.

Certainly, the doors have windows in them, so the library aides can make sure no one is making out or doing drugs, but other than that we're mostly safe to do as we please as long as we're not being ridiculous.

Technically we're *supposed* to be studying, but like the rest of the world, I am pretty sure in the history of high schools that No Student Ever has actually fully used study hall for its intended purpose, and that includes Goody Two-shoes like myself.

Liam, the college-age student aide who has a beard that would make lumberjacks jealous, pokes his head into our pod. "Are you all good to go for the day?" he asks with a goofy grin. His gaze pauses for a half second on Neta, and his ears turn pink.

Neta pauses from applying her lip gloss and spins around in her chair, crossing her legs. "Hi, Liam!" she says brightly. "How's your Comms project going?"

Neta has that effect on men, since she's basically a young Sofia Vergara. If she weren't so nice and if I were into that whole female-on-female jealousy thing (which I'm not, because I believe strong

SUCH A GOOD GIRL

women like Neta and me should support each other), it would be so easy to hate her. Plus, Neta is more than just a bombshell. She was just awarded a huge scholarship for being a Future Business-woman of America, and my bets are on her to become the next CEO of a huge company. Or to build one.

Liam gives Neta an awkward thumbs-up. "It's great, Neta. Thanks for asking. Listen, if you ever need help with your papers, I'm here. And that goes for you two as well, okay?" He points at Kolbie and me, and then strokes his beard, twisting his fingers into the end. "Well, later."

Kolbie grabs Neta's notebook and doodles *LIAM + NETA = FOREVER* on the cover in bright purple pen.

"Seriously? Are we in third grade?" Neta snips, but her mouth sort of quirks up, like she's trying not to laugh.

"My penmanship is on point." Kolbie doodles a little heart after "forever."

"Pretty sure he's just into me because you wouldn't give him the time of day," Neta says, reaching into her purse and pulling out her own pen. "Besides, Liam is sweet in a plaid sort of way. A girl could work with that." She yanks her notebook away from Kolbie.

I stand up and peer over her shoulder. "Then why are you scrawling over your statement of your eternal and lasting love?"

Neta swirls around to face us both, and displays the notebook. She's scribbled out the heart and replaced it with *BFF*. "You know what I say. I like to take it slow. Give love a real chance to develop between two mature people."

"Not me," Kolbie declares. "When I met Jamal, I basically knew

13

in, like, two seconds. We moved fast. Not like snail over here." She pushes on Neta's chair with her foot, spinning her in a circle.

"Hey!" Neta protests. "At least I'm not Little Miss Riley Stone, who makes Queen Elizabeth look easy."

"Don't drag me into this." I put a hand over my chest. "Besides, everyone knows Queen Elizabeth was a total badass. Don't hate. Besides, I'm like Neta. I would take it slow if I met someone anyway."

Kolbie bites on the tip of her pen and raises an eyebrow a little evilly. "Just saying. You don't like to take it at all is what I heard."

"I'm choosy!" I protest, but we're all laughing so hard, Liam knocks on the door.

"Can you girls keep it down a little? Or maybe turn on some music so the others aren't disturbed?" He smiles apologetically.

"Sorry, Liam." Neta pouts. "Don't let this come between us!" she calls after him as the door shuts.

Kolbie pulls a Bluetooth speaker out of her backpack and sets it on the desk. She puts on The Features and then kicks her red sneakers up on the table.

"Where'd you get that?" I ask, picking up the speaker and turning it over. It's definitely an upgrade from using an iPhone. I've seen it before. It's the newest model of a speaker that was just put out by a rapper turned mogul, and it's definitely out of my price range. "Damn, Kolbie. This is a nice one."

"Mom let me use a little money from the Zappos campaign." Kolbie makes a face. "She made me put the rest in a college fund."

She says "college fund" like everyone else says "poison" or

SUCH A GOOD GIRL

worse, "acid-wash jeans." Like she would never possibly have any use for a college fund.

Kolbie is also a supermodel. Well, almost. She's six one and was discovered at a coffee shop when she went to New York for the weekend with her mom. This man in what Kolbie calls ultra-skinny jeans and a long yellow scarf slipped her mother his business card, and the next thing you know she had an agent and was being jet-setted to photo shoots for magazines and stuff. And of course she's gorgeous, in this way that only magazine and runway models are that's a little bit seraphic. Her hair is always this huge explosion of curls and she has these perfect teeth that it looks like she had made and her outfits are always on point. It's all very effortless, like she just rolled into some clothes and they stuck on her and turned into art.

Needless to say, Kolbie is very glam and high fashion, and if she wasn't already a high school It Girl, a modeling contract would have made her one.

Anyway, as soon as she graduates from high school, her serious boyfriend, Jamal, is transferring to NYU, and she's moving straight to Manhattan to pursue her modeling career. She's already making some serious dough. She promised her mom to do college on the side, but honestly, I don't think she's serious about it. And who would be if they had a major modeling contract? Besides, she can go to college at any age . . . but how often can you go to Paris and be in the "Teens Who Rock" issue of *Claire?* Kolbie told us last week she gets a full-page spread and they're paying her five thousand dollars. When Neta and I found

15

out, we planned Kolbie a full spa day to celebrate (totally on us, of course), and I bought her a two-year subscription to the magazine.

"So, Neta," Kolbie says, "now that RJ is out of the picture, who's up to bat?" She picks at a little thread on the edge of her jeans. She likes her jeans perfectly frayed and is always tattering hers with pairs of scissors or trying to get the holes shredded just well enough that only a tiny bit of skin shows through.

Neta sighs heavily. "RJ."

"What's so great about RJ?" I cut in. "Didn't he basically cheat on you with Lorna Chatsworth over the summer?"

"They almost kissed."

"Because you interrupted them," Kolbie points out. "And who knows how many other almost-things they did or didn't do? Or actually did? There were totally rumors about RJ and Simone. And RJ and Gabriella, too. Don't forget those."

Neta pulls her business book out of her backpack. "Please. It's not like I'm going to take him back. I just like seeing him grovel. And I'm just saying I'm not quite over him."

"Neta—"

I reach forward to touch her shoulder, but she pushes my hand off with a small smile. "We were together since middle school, you know? It's hard to get over someone like that. You just hope that . . . that you mean more to someone than that."

Kolbie chews on the end of her pencil thoughtfully. "I get that. But in the meantime, distract yourself with something. Or some-one, if at all possible. Let's see." She stands and walks to the win-

SUCH A GOOD GIRL

dow of the door, peering out at the library. "Who's the hottest guy in the school? Let's start there."

Neta doesn't hesitate. "R—"

Kolbie cuts Neta off with a look. "Don't even think about him."

She sits back in her chair and sulks. "I was going to say, 'Are you serious?' Can't I just concentrate on ROIs for once?" She flashes us her business homework, which I happen to know she's already aced.

"Really selling that, Neta." I pat her on the shoulder and join Kolbie at the window. "There's Donovan. The quarterback. I know it's cliché, but it's very all-American high school." He's sitting near the magazine section, but he's paging through a thickish book. He's a pretty smart dude. He did an extra-credit speech last year on James Joyce that earned him serious academic cred in my book, especially considering the rest of the football team did their speeches on stuff like MMA fighting and cafeteria food.

"Boring." Kolbie nudges me. "Ooh, what about November?"

I follow her gaze. November is a hipster type whose real name is Francis Hastings Lee, but ever since he took up the guitar he insists on being called specifically *November* and nothing else.

Which, I will admit, I thought was the most diva-ish thing I'd ever heard until I listened to him play his guitar. He's actually incredible. There are rumors that three separate record labels are courting him, but I don't know if that's true. Still, he has a track or two up on iTunes, and his YouTube channel has more than two hundred thousand hits. That's saying something.

"I don't feel like competing with groupies," Neta says. "Besides,

17

you guys can stop looking out that window. If we're going purely by looks, it's really obvious, isn't it?"

Kolbie sighs heavily and turns toward Neta, resting her back against the door. "Yes," she says. "No contest."

"Uh, no." I look at Neta and Kolbie. "Who? Am I missing something? I think we've covered all the standouts."

"Mr. Belrose," they say together, as if it's the most obvious answer in the world.

Ah.

Mr. Belrose.

Our French teacher.

Our extremely attractive, jawline of a Greek god French teacher.

Key word "teacher."

He actually looks like he stepped off of a television show and just magically appeared in our classroom in a stylish button-up. I don't get it. There's no denying he's absolutely the most gorgeous man in a hundred-mile radius.

"I didn't know faculty was eligible."

"Oh," Neta says, giggling, "he's eligible, all right." Her cheeks get a touch rosy. "I mean, seriously, is there anyone that even compares?" She fans herself with her ROIs assignment.

"Nope," Kolbie says.

"Not even close," Neta says. "There's a reason why our school has the highest French scores in the state. And it's probably because every straight girl in the school—and some of the guys—sign up for his classes."

SUCH A GOOD GIRL

"And maybe because he's a really good teacher." I put my hands on my hips. "Besides, shouldn't there be some sort of age limit in place?"

Kolbie puts up a finger. "You are the biggest prude I have ever heard of, Riley. He's at *most* twenty-eight. Like, tops. We fangirl over celebs who are, like, eighty-six."

"That's pushing it."

She gives me a withering look. "You know what I mean."

She's not wrong. He is super young for a teacher. I'm pretty sure he only graduated from college four years ago. Or maybe less than that—not that long ago he was student teaching for the old French teacher, Mr. Andersen-Kraus.

"He's twenty-six," Neta says. "Same as your brother, Ri. They were in the same class."

She's not wrong.

"Regardless of age, he's mad altruistic," Kolbie points out. "Didn't he raise, like, ten thousand dollars for the cancer run last year?"

"And he volunteers at the hospital in his spare time, reading to children and, like, bandaging their little heads and stuff," Neta adds. "He's literally the perfect man."

I shake my head. "If only he wasn't married, right? You forget he's wifed up." I wiggle my ring finger.

Neta shakes her head, hair bouncing. "Come on, Riley. Loosen up. It's not like we're seriously considering a *teacher*. We're just fantasizing."

Kolbie thumps back in her chair and throws her feet up on the desk. "Seriously. You can't even admit he's fine, can you?"

19

"He's, um, a very nice-looking man."

"A very nice-looking man," Neta says in a high, squeaky voice, and they both crack up.

"For real? Are you trying to imitate me or Kermit the Frog?" I pretend to throw my chem book at her, and suddenly I'm laughing again too.

The door swings open while I'm fake-clobbering Neta and Liam stops, his eyes wide. "Um, excuse me," he says. "You know I think you girls are cool, but please, quiet down. And Riley, please don't assault anyone."

I clutch my book to my chest and suck my cheeks in to keep from smiling. "They should really put that in the library rules if they want it to be top of mind, Liam."

He nods. "I'll think about having signs put up," he says, completely dry.

We wait until he's closed the door to collapse in laughter again.

"This year," Neta announces, wiping away tears, "is the year of Hook Riley Up." She stands and holds up a bright pink pen and touches me on the nose with it, like she's knighting me or something. "You will get a boyfriend, or I will die trying. Or so help me God. Or whatever."

I back away. "Oh, no, no, no. I'm all set."

Kolbie clutches her hair. "That is so *boring*, Riley. Check yourself, girl. You're, like, incredibly smart, super funny, and mega hot." She checks off my dating qualifications on her fingers. "Like, one hundred and twelve percent of the guys in the school would date

SUCH A GOOD GIRL

you. Not to mention Jamal's college friends. And you could use a college guy. They're way more mature."

I straighten my blazer. "I have priorities that are more important than men. Like *actual* college, not just the men who attend the institution."

"Haven't you already gotten in to, like, eight schools?" Kolbie says. "Plus, not sure if you noticed, but men are *fun*. And if you get a good one instead of a douche-wrangler like RJ—"

"Hey!" Neta scowls.

"You know I'm right. Anyway, it's the best thing ever. Jamal is a good dude, and he makes me happier every day, you know?"

Something in my chest twists a little bit, and I think about Ethan and Esther, and how weird and messed up and perfect they are together.

And for all of Ethan's mistakes, how much more my parents seem to like him than me. It's like whenever the two of us are around, both of them just gravitate to him. Like he is easier to be around, in spite of the fact I did everything right and Ethan . . . well.

Ethan is Ethan.

"Come on, Riley!" Neta urges. She puts her arm around me. "It'll be fun! We can double-date or something!"

I put my hand on Neta's shoulder. "Look. I appreciate you guys. I do. But as soon as I graduate, I'm out of here. A man will only slow me down. And since when do I need a man? I'm a strong, powerful woman. I don't need anyone!" I make a muscle like Rosie the Riveter.

Kolbie sighs and puts her chin on her fist. "I didn't ever say you needed a man, Riles. I just said you needed some fun."

"I'm way fun," I insist. "Buckets of it."

"Oh yeah?" Neta counters. "When's the last time you broke a rule?"

"Stick with me. I'm totally going to chew gum in class later." I wink.

Neta throws up her hands, reminding me of my mother when she's annoyed. "You're hopeless, Ri. But I'm not giving up on you. You'll go on at least one date this year."

For about two seconds, I play with the normal teenage girl hope that rises up in my chest. Maybe dating someone wouldn't be so bad.

Then I pinch it out like a candle.

I am more than all of that.

THREE
Lessons

"Bonjour, la classe," Mr. Belrose says from the front of the classroom. He is holding a stack of papers loosely in one arm, and smiles at his students as they file in.

There's something about his voice.

Something different from everyone else.

Something about *him.*

The something gives me shivers just under my skin.

I give my head a little shake.

Thea Arnold, a senior with a penchant for wearing entirely too much jewelry, pauses at the front of the classroom. *"Bonjour,* Monsieur Belrose," she drawls, her words drawn out and slow and deliberately flirty. Her friends giggle beside her and all choose seats in the front row, nearest to his desk, where they cross and uncross their legs and make pouty faces and apply shiny lip gloss.

"*Bonjour*, Thea." He nods at her and she slides into her customary seat right in front of his desk.

Mr. Belrose is cool like that. He lets everyone choose their seats every day. He isn't like one of those teachers who has assigned seating. Of course, most of the girls choose seats in the front row. Except me. I think it's a little desperate. I do get it. They all know that they're never going to actually be with a beautiful married teacher, so they're just in it for the best view possible, but even so—I'm perfectly happy with the third row. Close enough that I can still see what's going on, but not so far back that I look like a total slacker.

As soon as most of the class is seated, Mr. Belrose begins handing out papers.

"What is this?" Thea asks immediately, her voice slightly accusatory. She might like Mr. Belrose, but she's not the most academic girl around. I've heard rumors, though, that her grades are strictly on account of laziness and she's been tested and is secretly a Mensa-level genius, which is how she made it into honors senior French.

"*En français,*" Mr. Belrose says. His voice is—interesting. He's demanding it, and we all know it, but it's sort of . . . well, soft. And inviting. And . . .

I am not into Mr. Belrose. I am not. I am into studies. And responsibility. And maybe a couple of celebs. Not teachers. Not educators. Not men who wear smart button-ups and have rich, clever voices and—

SUCH A GOOD GIRL

"Qu'est-ce que c'est?" Thea says, very slowly.

Mr. Belrose grins. *"Une interrogation surprise!"*

I perk up. I *own* at surprise quizzes. In fact, I've aced every single pop quiz that Belrose has ever thrown my way.

Garrett, a star baseball player behind me, pretends to choke.

His buddy Cay hits him in the arm. "Dude! Come on! *En français!"*

The whole class bursts out laughing. *"Un crédit supplementaire pour Monsieur Burke!"* Mr. Belrose grins and makes a flourish at Cay Burke.

That's just another reason why everyone loves Mr. Belrose. He's got a great sense of humor. Every other teacher probably would have been annoyed at Cay's joke, but Mr. Belrose actually gave him extra credit. Sure, it'll probably be only one point, but how cool is that?

A piece of paper lands on my desk and I glance over it. It looks pretty easy . . . just a review of verbs. Old ones too. Sometimes Belrose does this. He throws weeks-old stuff at us, just so we remember it. He doesn't want us to recall the language long enough for a test and then clear it out as soon as new material comes along. He wants us to retain French. He wants us to learn it as he has learned it, so we can stroll along the streets of Paris and order *macarons* and ride bicycles around with baguettes perched jauntily on our shoulders. Typical French activities.

I fill in the verbs quickly as Belrose walks up and down the aisles of desks and tsks at some papers and whispers, *"Très bien!"* over people's shoulders. He's rather distracting, all in all, during test taking. I finish with mine first and walk my paper up to his

25

desk. He catches my eye as he leans over Teri Von Millhouse's desk and winks at me.

Pursing my lips, I turn my back to him and saunter back to my seat, keeping my shoulders square and tall. My eyes stray to the photos of the Seine he has on the walls; copies of the paintings hung in the Louvre; lovely aerial photos of the French Riviera, and one tiny, cliché photo of the Eiffel Tower, which is a requirement in any respectable French classroom. I do not look back at Mr. Belrose.

I do not care about my French teacher.

I don't. Not like *that*. It takes more than a pretty face and an infallible French accent to sway me. It does not matter that he winks at me and pays more attention to me than to other students.

I do, of course, care about my grade. And I care about *Les Mis*.

Speaking of which.

I sit back down at my desk and pull my copy of *Les Misérables* out of my backpack. I try to read, but my eyes stray back to Mr. Belrose as he returns to his desk to grade the quizzes. He doesn't get to mine right away, because it was the first one turned in, and therefore on the bottom of the pile, so he makes a lot of strikes with his red pen before he reaches my paper, where he makes one mark: an A.

It's not like I can see it from here. But I recognize the three sharp strokes, like the Eiffel Tower.

I smile tightly to myself and bite on the cap of my pen.

A few minutes later, Mr. Belrose rises from his desk and passes copies of the tests back to the class.

"*Classe*, I'm going to switch to English for a few minutes while

SUCH A GOOD GIRL

we review the quiz together, and you're going to tell me the verbs in French. Let's start with, ah, Thea."

Thea glows.

"'To make.'"

"Faire," Thea recites. Her accent is far from on point, but she does tend to have her French down.

I wonder why.

"Correct." Mr. Belrose rewards her with a smile, and she lights up like fireworks. He moves to the second word. "Uh, let's go with . . . Riley. Riley, how do you say 'to kiss'?"

Suddenly, I feel redness in my cheeks. Of course the word "kiss" is incredibly close to the word "embarrass," which he is currently doing. To me. *"Embrasser."*

"No one's surprised that Riley's correct!" He smiles even bigger at me than he did at Thea and then moves on to someone else, and my cheeks heat up even brighter. I duck my head, letting my hair fall in front of my face, praying that no one is looking at me.

I do not care about Mr. Belrose. I do not.

"You okay under there, Stone?" Garrett asks, poking me in the soft space just below my shoulder with the eraser end of his pencil.

I ignore him. I ignore everyone, even after the crimson in my cheeks has gone away and the bell rings and I've ignored about fourteen questions I definitely could have answered better than anyone else in the class. I shove my books into my backpack quickly and start toward the door, using my blond hair as a nice, effective curtain in front of my face.

"Mademoiselle Stone? *S'il vous plaît, attendez.*"

27

He wants me to wait. Mr. Belrose wants me to wait.

I think about the monks in Asia or somewhere who can control their bodies to a point where they can slow down their pulse simply by concentrating. I wish for that power now.

I turn slowly toward Mr. Belrose. *"Oui?"*

His faces softens from the normal teacher expression he wears—all the stern planes and angles smoothed out into something almost friendly. "I've been meaning to talk to you about something. Do you have a moment?"

I shift my backpack. I didn't position my books right, and the corner of my French book digs into the back of my right hip. "Yes?" My heart is beating unevenly with him so close. I am attracted to him.

I think of his hands on me.

My God. I need to get it together.

His eyes shift behind me. "Uh, actually, you know, I'll just catch up with you next class, okay? Great job on the quiz, though, Riley. You've retained a lot of information this year."

I squint at him, but he's still looking behind me. I turn—and see one of the new basketball players, a transfer from across town, waiting behind me to talk to Mr. Belrose.

Huh.

Whatever Belrose was going to say to me . . . he didn't want to say it in front of someone else.

Something in my stomach does an odd little jump, but I tamp it down.

Whatever he was going to say . . . it doesn't matter.

SUCH A GOOD GIRL

Not one bit.

I square my shoulders and walk out of the classroom.

I wouldn't flirt with him. And he couldn't flirt with me. I'm not like Thea. It's different with Mr. Belrose and me. We have . . . a history.

He is, after all, the same age as my brother.

I walk down the hallway to my locker, where I spin the combination without thinking and change out my books, which are all lined up neatly and have color-coded book covers for each class.

Mr. Belrose has helped me before.

He hasn't always been a teacher.

There was a time when he was just my brother's friend and I knew him as Alex and he was just the cute youth counselor helping out at the church, where we raised money each year to donate to domestic violence shelters. There was a time when I didn't think too much about talking to him, when his hair wasn't brushed so carefully and he didn't wear neatly buttoned shirts and khakis and he cursed a lot more. It was before he'd studied abroad in France his senior year of college and met Jacqueline and gotten married to someone who looked like she'd been painted by an impressionist.

I remember one time in particular.

With Alex. Not Mr. Belrose. Not then, at least.

I was volunteering. Because volunteering is part of me. It's more than just a résumé; if I really listed all my charity work on my CV, I'd have to cut down a good portion of a forest just for the paper.

That day, I was collecting clothes for domestic violence victims. My mother and I had gone through her overcrowded closet the night before, and I'd had fun trying on her high heels while she sorted through her old shirts and made startled noises about how she used to dress.

"Are you sure the women will even want these?" she had asked me, holding up a sweater with a tiny robin sewn onto the pocket. She wrinkled her nose. "We don't want to *insult* them."

And I wobbled over on a pair of her highest stilettos that she refused to donate but also swore were too uncomfortable to wear and added the robin sweater to her Donate pile. "It's fine."

It had taken hours, but I'd ended up struggling with a giant black trash bag of clothing. Mr. Belrose (Alex at the time) had seen me come through the door with it, my legs nearly buckling under the weight of it all. He tried to take the bag from me, but I held my hand out. "I got it." I walked unsteadily back to the booth we were both assigned to and heaved the bag behind the table.

He grinned at me the whole way, and I wasn't sure if he thought I was being silly by refusing the help or if he was sort of impressed, but I chose to believe the latter, and that I was one of those plucky sort of independent girls who people admired. It wasn't until I turned around and wiped my sweaty hair out of my eyes (I had some truly ill-advised bangs at that stage of my life) that his smile hit a false note.

"Looking a little rough there, Riley."

His eyes held mine—my left one, specifically, which was a messy watercolor of purple and black.

I let myself smile as much as my face allowed. The pain wasn't terrible, but it was always there, a constant reminder. The previous

SUCH A GOOD GIRL

night, during a basketball game, I'd gotten elbowed by a girl who looked more like a female Thor than an eighth grader.

So I hadn't made the layup.

And only one of the two free throws, because I couldn't see through my eye for the second one.

(Shortly after, I'd decided cheerleading full time was more my speed.)

"Bad night," I muttered, pulling open the trash bag. "How are we sorting these, anyway?"

"Uh, shoes, pants, shirts. And then by size. What sizes do you have here?"

I pulled out a pink turtleneck. "This is a medium. I think my mom was, like, a six back then, though."

"Okay." Alex bent down to grab an armful of clothes from the garbage bag and began going through them, tossing them into piles without folding them.

A woman with an oversize banana clip clamped into her hair came to the table with a musty box. "I got clothes," she said. "Can I drop these here?"

"You're at the right place." I tried to smile at her, but she just sort of chewed her gum in my direction.

"Can you give me a receipt for my taxes?"

I stared at her. "Uh—"

"If you can't, I'll just take 'em back home." She put her arms around the box. "There's lots of good stuff in here."

Alex popped up beside me, one of my mother's paisley sweaters still draped over his arm. "I can take care of that." He tossed the

31

sweater at me. "Riley, you're on sort duty." He grinned at me and pulled a pad of paper out of his back pocket.

I turned to my mom's garbage bag, and a minute later, Alex was back with the musty box. He opened it, and a puff of dust came off the top. "So," he said very quietly, so that no one at the booths on either side of us would hear, "can I ask you something really serious?"

I looked up at him and nodded, and for some reason, my pulse was going crazy. I could hear thudding in my ears, like pulling up beside a car with the bass turned up too high.

"Sure." My voice was barely above a whisper.

He reached down and grabbed an airy lavender silk scarf. He wrapped it around his neck and put his hand on my shoulder. "Is this—is this my color?" His lip quivered with a held-back smirk.

I cracked up. Pain shot through my face, but I couldn't help it. "Nope," I said, yanking the scarf away. It left his neck with a sharp *snick* sound as the fabric slid across his skin.

"What's going on here?" A familiar voice cut through my laughter, and we both turned.

Ethan.

Ethan, looking . . . all too familiar. His untidy hair was sticking up on one side like he had fallen asleep against something, and from the smell emanating off him . . . he had been drinking. Again.

A lot.

"You're early." My voice was frosty but calm. Very calm. "You weren't supposed to pick me up for another hour."

"Hey, man." Alex and Ethan did the sort of half-hug-and-hit thing that guys do. Only Ethan's half was wobbly. "You okay?"

SUCH A GOOD GIRL

Ethan shook his head like he was trying to clear it. "Uh, yeah. You got a chair or something?"

Alex and I exchanged a quick look. We couldn't really have a drunk dude hanging out at a domestic violence table. "Uh, yeah. Listen, how about you lie down back here for a minute?" Alex grabbed my brother's arm and guided him back, behind the largest piles of clothes, and put a couple of hoodies on the floor. Ethan stretched out on top of them and balled up a flowery blouse as a pillow.

"Think he'll pass out?" Alex whispered as he climbed from behind the piles of clothes.

I nodded. "He probably already has. Unless he snores, we're golden."

An older man with a cane approached the table, and Alex helped him while I snuck a look at my brother. His eyes were already closed, and his mouth had the slightly open look of sleep.

I grabbed a body spray from my purse and misted it in his direction, hoping no one close could smell the alcohol on him. I didn't want anyone to see my brother like that. Think of him like that.

He was better. He deserved better. Something was just going on with him lately, and I didn't understand. No one did. He came home late and he slept in late and he didn't talk to me anymore. But this wasn't him.

Still, he was definitely not going to be sober in an hour. Or anytime tonight. I was going to have to find another way home. And it wasn't just like I could call my parents. They were already pissed at Ethan. I didn't want to make it worse.

33

I sank down in a chair and slumped over, sighing. A few minutes later, Alex joined me, sitting cross-legged on the floor, below me. He looked up through his unkempt hair. "You okay?"

"Yep." The response was automatic and came out before I could think about how much of a complete lie it was. Maybe always was. It's one of those questions you're never really supposed to answer. Maybe it didn't count as a lie if you weren't ever supposed to tell the truth.

"Your eye—" He started to reach up, but then pulled his hand away, as if thinking better of it.

I nodded. "I know. It doesn't look good." I hesitated. "Things aren't . . . great."

I was misleading him and I knew it. He thought I was talking about my eye and I wasn't. I was talking about everything. Everything else. "I mean, this is fine," I amended, pointing at my eye. "Someone got a little aggressive with me during yesterday's game."

Alex just looked at me, the question in his face. But he was patient. He didn't push or prod, but he was still asking. I saw him asking.

"Things aren't always good at home." I looked back toward Ethan to make sure he wasn't stirring. "Ethan is always coming home blitzed. And my parents, they're angry, but he's just trying to make things easier. It's not like my dad doesn't drink too."

Alex's eyebrows shot up. "Your dad?"

I gave a tiny nod. "It gets a little scary. Sometimes I worry . . . he's not going to wake up. And my mom . . . she's just empty. She's hollow, like she's this perfect person on the outside and on the inside

SUCH A GOOD GIRL

she's, I don't know, not even a person anymore. None of us really are. We're like these plastic people and we look so perfect as long as you don't see where we've been molded together so carefully." I stopped suddenly, aware of how bitter I sounded. I glanced at the booth to the right, where there were three women working, to make sure they weren't paying attention. "You won't tell anyone, will you?"

I was laying it on a little thick, but I relished his attention.

He reached up and linked his pinkie with mine, like we were girls together at a sleepover, sharing secrets. "No."

I gave him a smile with the side of my face that didn't hurt. "Thanks."

We were quiet for a while, and no one paid attention to us, set up in a booth in the big gymnasium, his hand linked with mine.

"I know it sounds stupid and everyone always says it," he said finally, "but it's going to be okay."

And even though it did sound a little stupid, it was exactly what I needed to hear. I let myself believe him.

So I let Alex hold my hand, and at the end of the night, he helped Ethan to his car. On the way home, with Ethan stretched out across his backseat, he took my hand again and squeezed it, and even though he didn't say it, I could feel it when he touched me.

Everything was going to be all right.

FOUR
Shame

"Rob!"

Rob Samuels, a senior football player I've gone to school with since preschool, stands at the end of the hallway, talking with Mr. Peters, the chemistry teacher and offensive coordinator.

Rob and I used to be really close. We used to play together at recess almost every day, and we'd usually stake our claim on the tornado slide on the east side of the playground, farthest away from any teachers on duty. When I fell down the ladder one day, Rob helped me inside and bandaged my knee for me without letting any of the other kids see I was crying. And when we got to be captains during PE, Rob would always choose me first for his football team, no matter what. But when Rob got really good, and

SUCH A GOOD GIRL

I started hanging out with Neta and Kolbie, that kind of changed.
I kind of changed.

I don't follow the football team that closely anymore. I guess
I sort of lost touch. I show up and cheer, sure, and I know who
wins and loses, but my mind is elsewhere. I can reel off the players
mechanically, and even the plays, if needed, but that's just it . . . it's
automatic. I don't let myself love it.

Rob doesn't hear me.

"Hey, Rob!" I call again. I bounce on my toes and wave my
hand, and half the hall turns hopefully. Mr. Peters hears me and
says something inaudible to Rob, who turns.

His face splits into a wide grin.

Rob is glad to see me.

Always is.

Always has been.

That's how I knew I could count on him.

He waits on me at the end of the hallway, his backpack hanging
on one shoulder, the goofy smile on his face. "Hey, Riley."

"Hi, Rob. Hi, Mr. Peters."

Mr. Peters nods and gives Rob a little punch on the shoulder,
like, *Go get 'em, champ,* which I have no doubt has to do with me,
before vanishing back into his classroom. The action makes me
feel a little sick.

"What's up, Riley?" Rob asks. "What can I do for you?"

I cast a look back over my shoulder, at Belrose's classroom.

What can Rob do for me?

Because even Rob, smart, sandy-haired Rob, who a million girls

37

like, who already has two football scholarship offers to good schools, respected schools, is a little suspicious of why I'd be talking to him.

Riley Stone doesn't date.

Everyone knows that.

So there has to be another reason why I'd be talking to him.

And there is.

It's because of . . . that night.

With Alex.

With Belrose.

What happened that night was most definitely not Riley Stone.

Not even a young Riley Stone.

It was stupid.

It was vulnerable.

And it's because of that moment in the classroom last week.

Nothing like that can ever happen again. After all, I have a future to think about. And if that means I have to put up some sort of obstacle between the two of us, even if it's just for my own sake, then that's what I'll do.

I link my arm through Rob's and draw him close to my side. "Well, we used to be friends, didn't we, Rob?"

"Sure," he says, slowly, as if waiting for the punch line, but there's something else in his voice. Eagerness.

"I was just thinking about you. That's all." I make my voice a little shy. A touch quiet. I was just thinking about him. I'm not promising anything. But if I can walk past Belrose's classroom with him attached to me, then maybe it will convince me that I am not actually interested. And that he is not . . .

38

SUCH A GOOD GIRL

Anyway.

It'll be enough for both of us. It will need to be.

"Yeah?" Rob asks, a little more air in his voice than usual, and his arm tightens around my own. "Yeah?"

He does that a lot. Or at least he used to. Repeat himself.

"Yeah." I let myself agree. "What class do you have?"

"World history. What do you have?" He looks down at me, his eyes filled with wonder, like he absolutely can't believe his luck, and all around us, I can feel people looking. For a moment, I feel like a starlet, and not in a good way—in a way that I feel like people are invading, ready to snap photos, ready to whisper, ready to take stock of my life and lay it all out for entertainment, and I'm exploiting it, mapping out the story and the characters and setting for my own gain.

"Walk me to the library. I have study hall," I direct. "Let's catch up."

"Of course," he says, and he's still looking at me as this great mystery, but there's happiness behind it. He turns up the stairs.

"Wait," I say. "Where are you going?"

"Library."

Oh. He wants to take the shortcut, straight to the study pod where Kolbie, Neta, and I always meet, which is on the second floor of the library. But I need to walk past the French classroom.

"Do you mind if I go to my locker first?" I say, blinking a couple of extra times. I think it's true what they say about eyelashes. They're endearing. All Neta has to do is bat her long black eyelashes and guys are practically dog-piling at her feet.

39

AMANDA K. MORGAN

But that goes for anything Neta does. And has since basically fifth grade.

Rob walks with me to my locker, his chest puffed out and his shoulders squared. "Are you having a good day?" he asks me, and I realize, while I'm adding extra pencils that I don't actually need to my backpack, that he's waiting for my answer, his eyes wide.

He actually wants to know.

"Um, yes." It's automatic, like always. "Just the usual, you know? What about you?"

"Amazing." He looks at me, his gray eyes solemn, and I know he means it. "Just really great."

I smile at him, and my heart drops the tiniest bit in my chest. But I link arms with him again anyway, and he walks me toward the library, like he's supposed to be the man on my arm, and I feel the hallway buzzing around us, as if every single person is more interested in what's happening in my life than I am.

Except for the ten seconds when I walk past the French classroom. And in my peripheral vision, I see Mr. Belrose, in a cornflower-blue button-up, leaning against his door frame, talking to Lydia Andrews, one foot kicked up in front of the other.

And I think maybe, just for a second, he pauses when he sees me floating by with Rob. But I don't turn my head. After all, Mr. Belrose doesn't matter.

And maybe it's just my imagination, but I am almost certain I feel his eyes on my back as I walk away.

But I *don't* care. Not really.

"I have a football meeting tonight," Rob says apologetically as

40

SUCH A GOOD GIRL

we reach the wide glass doors of the library. "Otherwise I'd ask you to hang out."

"That's okay, Rob. I'll just see you tomorrow at school." I give him a careful, practiced smile, and he returns it in full force.

"This was nice."

I nod. "I appreciate it." I am being honest. I do.

Rob pauses, working over something in his mind. I know the look. He's about to ask me something. Something I don't really want. "Listen—"

The bell rings, cutting him short.

I pretend to panic, checking my cell phone for the time. "I gotta go. I'll catch you later, okay, Rob?"

I touch his arm softly and disappear into the library, and when I finally look back, he's still there, watching me from the glass doors, not caring that he's late. It doesn't matter if I'm late to study hall, but I happen to know that football players who are late to class usually have to run extra in their conditioning practices.

But he's still there, watching me, his mouth a little slack.

I give him a wave, and walk up the stairs toward the study pod, where Kolbie and Neta are waiting.

"What the hell, Ri?" Kolbie says immediately, showing me her cell phone. "Are you hooking up with Rob on the down low?"

There, on the screen, is a picture of me, my arm linked through Rob's. I'm looking straight ahead, my gaze carefully fixed in front of me, and Rob is looking down at me, like he can't quite believe I'm there.

"It's nothing." I settle into my chair and pull out my French

41

book, like I'm actually going to use the time to conjugate verbs or something. "Honestly, it's just old friends, walking to class together. And who sent you that?"

"I got two," Neta says. "This high school is disgusting. And you'd better be careful, Ri. That boy has got it bad for you. If you talk to him one more time, he might fall in love."

A short "ha" bursts out of Kolbie's throat. "Are you kidding me? Rob Samuels has been in love with Riley since preschool, when they built that Popsicle stick castle for art and Riley let him kiss her."

"Whoa, Riley. First kiss in preschool? Who would have thought?"

"It wasn't even her first," Kolbie says. "Riley kissed *everyone* in preschool. I mean *everyone*."

I start to laugh. "It was a serious problem. My dad had read me that story about that princess who kissed a frog and it turned into a prince, and I don't know, I got obsessed with kissing or something, and the next thing you know, both my parents were called in for a sit-down with the guidance counselor." I giggle. "It was an issue."

"Perfect Riley Stone, make-out maniac," Neta singsongs. "All I know is you better get a handle on this Rob situation. If it goes any further, he'll be hitting up your phone by the end of the week." Her phone vibrates on the desk, and she picks it up. "Oh look, another one!"

It's a picture of Rob and me, walking down the hall, with Belrose in the background.

He's looking away, obviously preoccupied with something else, failing to notice me walking down the hallway with someone on my arm.

SUCH A GOOD GIRL

Which is fine, of course.

"I'll handle it," I tell them.

And so that day, after school, I wait until the girls who have stupid questions about their French homework clear out of Mr. Belrose's classroom, and then I walk in. I stand in front of his desk for a moment, where he's sitting, a pair of black-framed reading glasses perched on his nose. They're very hipster and the frames are a little scraped, and I wonder if he needs them at all or if they're just for looks.

"Hello, Mr. Belrose."

He looks up, as if he's just noticing me, when I know for a fact the heels of my boots clicked very satisfyingly on the tiles when I walked in. "Oh, hey, Riley. Can I help you with something?" His forehead wrinkles, like he doesn't already know.

"I believe it was you who wanted to talk to me? Last class?" I keep my tone even. This is business. This is something that I need to have taken care of so I can stop thinking about it forever.

"Oh, right." He snaps his fingers, and pulls open his desk drawer. "I apologize, but I didn't want to do this in front of any other students. It might cause jealousy, you know. I'm sure you understand."

Mr. Belrose comes up a moment later with two crisp white pieces of paper, fastened neatly together with a tiny black binder clip. "You're the only student I'm giving this to, Riley. It's the Lou F. Durand Scholarship, and it's only for those who are interested in continuing their education in French in college. It's only for the most exceptional of students. Now, you don't have to major in

43

it, but I believe you have to commit to taking at least two college courses, and this will pay for a semester of study abroad. Are you interested?"

My heart twists and beats and burns. This is everything and nothing I expected. A semester in France? More money for college? Of course. I would love a semester in France.

I force my face into a smile. *"Oui,"* I say. *"Merci."*

"Of course, Riley." He smiles back at me and takes off the glasses. "You'll get it. I knew as soon as I read it that this scholarship was for you. You'd make a perfect French teacher, you know."

"Would I?" I ask. I don't want to be a French teacher. I'm not sure what I want to do, honestly, but it's not that. I've made up a million different things and career paths in my college applications, but I'm not actually sure I mean any of them. Still, he paid me a genuine compliment. "Thank you."

Mr. Belrose extends his hand toward me, the papers clasped in it, and when I reach to take them, the skin of his hand brushes mine, just for a second.

It's not electric, like books say. It's not a shock. But it's warm, and nice, and there's—there's something there. A current, like there's already a bond. Something that I didn't feel when Rob intertwined his arm with mine.

"Have a good night, okay?" Belrose says, turning back to the papers on his desk.

Like he didn't feel anything at all. But he had to. A bond like that is felt between two people, not one. But he's playing professional.

44

SUCH A GOOD GIRL

"You too. Thanks, Mr. Belrose." I tuck the papers into a folder, slide it into my backpack, and I turn to walk away.

"You and Rob, huh?" he asks quietly, as I'm halfway to the door.

Bingo. I smile to myself. "Maybe."

And I realize maybe my little plan wasn't so fruitless after all.

That night, I dream of Rob. I dream of Rob and me and Popsicles, and we're talking and laughing and walking, and we're having fun, real fun, like I thought I never could have with him, and I'm thinking about how his eyelashes are sandy like his hair. But then when he leans in to kiss me it's not Rob anymore.

It's Alex.

Not Mr. Belrose.

But Alex, from the booth, who linked pinkies with me and held my hand in the car. Alex, who was nice and a little wild and fun. Alex, who was more a sleepy college student, half awake for class, than my teacher.

And he was nice to kiss.

Things to Know About Riley Stone:

- In second grade, Riley was the starting quarterback for the Pee-Wee football team. Her father was incredibly proud.
- Her mother made her quit in third grade and enrolled her in cheerleading and gymnastics.
- Riley won every spelling bee she ever entered. Every. Single. One.
- By age ten, Riley was so used to winning that she started making participation trophies for all the other students just so they wouldn't feel bad. She made special ones for her brother, because he never seemed to win at anything he entered.
- Riley always wanted to enter child beauty pageants, but her parents forbid it.
- They did, however, allow her to become a child model when she was discovered at an Applebee's while adorably covered in ice cream. She was even featured in a national ad at age four.

FIVE
Escape

"You're here."

Ethan steps back from his door, his brow furrowed.

"Yeah. Can I come in?" I peer inside his apartment, but it looks almost black inside, like maybe I'd woken him from a nap. The only light is a soft flickering, probably from the television. "I mean, is Esther here or something?"

He shakes his head. "No, she's at her parents' house. Come in if you want. Just . . . what are you doing here?" Ethan stands aside to let me in his apartment.

I walk past him. His modest TV is the source of the flickering, and the whole place smells like stale corn chips and Febreze. "I needed to get out of the house. It was suffocating me." I settle down onto the couch, next to a pile of laundry. I can't tell if it's clean or dirty.

"That's why I moved out so fast," Ethan says, grinning. "It's not like I'm not thankful for our upper-middle-class upbringing, but that house is sometimes the smallest place in the world."

He understands. My brother understands. I want to hug him. I nod instead.

"Do you want a beer or something?" he asks.

I shake my head. "Water is fine, if you have it."

Ethan disappears into the kitchen and comes back with a bottle full of grocery store brand water, which I accept gratefully. He flops back into his recliner. It looks about ten years old, which is saying something, considering I've never seen it before. And I've even been here once, when he first moved in after college.

"I would have straightened up if I knew you were coming," he says, twisting the top off his own beer. He pitches it in the direction of the kitchen, and I hear it clatter on the floor.

I laugh. "No, you wouldn't have."

He grins. "You're right. Still, I might have pushed the clothes onto the floor or something. Besides, it's not like you came over here in your Sunday best." He eyes my sweats and HARTSVILLE HIGH CHEER SQUAD T-shirt.

"Hey," I protest. "I came straight from cheerleading practice."

"And you smell like it."

I resist rolling my eyes. I know my ponytail is a sweaty mess that I've sort of pushed on my head and fastened with a hair tie, but he's my brother. It's written into the laws of family that

SUCH A GOOD GIRL

unless it's Thanksgiving, and your great-granny Beatrice who you haven't seen in two years is visiting, you don't have to dress to impress anybody because they're genetically forced to love you. "Whatever."

"Do you want to watch something on TV?" Ethan offers, trying to be a halfway decent host. He makes to throw the remote at me, but I hold up my hand.

"Whatever is good." I don't really watch television. I don't have time for it, exactly, outside of a few juicy reality shows that you don't exactly have to keep up with to understand.

I am preoccupied with more important things.

My brother has a basketball game on, and we watch together, in silence, for a few minutes in his strange-smelling apartment. He's just *happy*. Like fully got-it-together, all-the-time happy. It's not like his job pays him well, or that he's even figured out how the hell he's going to help raise another man's baby, but he loves Esther and Esther loves him back and he's pretty content with that.

He doesn't need anything else.

It's not like he hasn't screwed up a million times. He has. He's been in trouble with school, his grades, my parents, the police, but here he is, in his little apartment, with his secondhand (or maybe thirdhand) furniture . . . and he's completely got it together.

More than I do.

And if you're going by the book, I've got it together. Of course I do.

"Are you okay?"

"What?" I ask.

51

Ethan's not watching the basketball game. "You just . . . you look sort of . . . tense, Riley. Is there something going on?"

"I'm fine." I smooth down my already smooth hair.

"That," Ethan says, pausing to take a sip of his beer, "is a dead giveaway."

"Of what?" I demand, forcing my hand back into my lap. I am not fidgeting. I am calm.

"That something is not right."

"Everything is fine," I snap. "It's just, I don't understand how you can be so happy all the goddamned time with so much stressful shit going on in your life."

Ethan cocks his head at me. "What stressful shit?"

"A pregnant girlfriend? Not your baby? A job that doesn't pay enough? A record? I mean, does any of this ring a bell?"

Ethan shakes his head. "Riley. First of all, why does any of that actually matter? My job pays enough to cover my bills and a little extra. I'm saving for the baby. Second of all, my girlfriend makes me happy. And third, it's not like I was a real criminal. So honestly . . . what do I really have to be worried about, at the end of the day? What's in my life that actually, genuinely needs fixing?"

He says this all calmly, like I haven't just accidentally insulted his entire existence. He pauses for a moment, and the sound of the basketball game fills the room: the announcers, the cheering, and the buzzer for halftime and the traffic passing outside. The stoplights shine faintly into the living room window: red, green, yellow, and red again. It's maddening and calming all at once, the way the lights hit the floor at the edge of the recliner.

SUCH A GOOD GIRL

Ethan leans forward. "Are you projecting, Riley?"

I lift a shoulder in a shrug, something I'd never dare do in a classroom.

Ethan continues, "Because I think you're worried you need fixing. And you don't know how to do it. And maybe you're not happy. And maybe that's because you're in high school, and high school's hard and it sucks and teenage angst and blah, blah, blah. Or maybe"—Ethan pauses, leans back in his chair, and takes a sip of beer—"you just need to practice not giving a shit for once in your entire life."

"Um, excuse me?" I say, very quietly. For some reason, I feel strange, and a little drowsy, and completely out of place. Maybe someone's going to pop out and shake me. No one talks to me like Ethan when we're alone. No one.

I wouldn't let them.

"There's this idea that you have to plan out your life perfectly before you go to college, and it's like this giant set of dominos: if you knock one over, you're totally screwed and they're all gone. But it's not, Riley. You need to relax every once in a while. And if you let something slide, so what? You've got a million other shiny gold stars on your résumé that'll back you up. They're not going anywhere."

I stare at my brother, in his sweats and holey T-shirt, sitting cross-legged on the old recliner. "Are you, like, moonlighting as an inspirational speaker? Or—"

"Shut your face." He throws a smelly pillow at me. "I'm trying to be your brother."

I grab his laundry and throw it back at him, mostly so I won't

53

have to sit next to it anymore. And I ask about his new video game, which is the only luxury stuff he actually spends real money on, aside from things for Esther.

But inside, I think about what he's saying.

He basically wants me to pull a Sandy from *Grease*. But I can't just do the things that everyone else just wants to do. It gives me anxiety. I can't enjoy it the way other people can, and God, I wish I could. I wish I could just let go.

But my brother is saying it'll be the thing that'll make me happy.

But what if I did relax? Just the smallest bit.

"Anyway," he says, "how's everything else going? How's school?"

"It's kind of boring. Everyone's still there. Oh, an old friend of yours is teaching." I say this very casually, because it is, of course, a very casual conversation that I have no stake in.

"Really?" A commercial for detergent comes on, so Ethan switches to another channel. "Who?"

"Alex Belrose. He's teaching French."

"French?" Ethan snorts. "Really? I always thought he'd be more of the kindergarten type." He says it with condescension. Ethan clearly doesn't remember the Alex who threw him on old clothes because he was too drunk to function and then drove us home, and I'm not about to remind him. I don't want to chance him remembering—other things. Hand-holding things.

Past-things-that-need-to-stay-there things.

"Nope. I'm in his class."

Ethan chuckles. "I bet that's a goddamned mess."

SUCH A GOOD GIRL

"Um, what do you mean?" I keep my tone normal. I don't care. I shouldn't.

"He just doesn't seem like the academic type, that's all."

"Really? I mean, I'm in his honors senior French, you know. He doesn't *completely* suck. Of course, he's not exactly the best teacher out there." I feel a little bad saying that. Mr. Belrose is actually really good. He cares, I think, or maybe he's just not burned-out yet. He wants everyone to learn and grow and care about the language the same way he does. No one has done anything so horrible during class that it has irrevocably scarred him. Yet. And he's been tempted by about every girl in the school, and I don't actually think he's given in. He's a good guy.

Ethan laughs. "That's what I meant. In high school he was just a ladies' man. He had a new girl, like, every week. And in college he was always too stoned to worry about girls. I lost touch with him. I didn't know he graduated." Ethan stops on an MMA channel where two huge guys are pummeling each other. One has blood in his eyeball. "Whatever, I guess. He was just kind of a weird dude."

I want to ask more, but I stop myself. I cannot give my stake in this away. "Yeah." I take a sip of my water. The grocery brand is always a little oily and sits on my tongue even after I swallow, but it's better than tap.

"Side note," he says, "Esther's little sister says you're dating Rob Samuels. I think I should meet him."

I shake my head. "No," I say. "That, you're wrong about."

"Meeting him or dating him?"

I don't meet his eyes. "Both."

55

SIX
Bad

The bell rings, the sound dulled only slightly between the thick stacks of books in the library.

Not the first bell. The second one. And this isn't study hall, where Liam wouldn't dare mark me late, either. This is Shakespeare, where Mrs. Hamilton is well known for having a rather sizeable stick up her ass.

It won't matter, though. I'm never late. Ever. And I have to do this. I have to *try* it. To see if Ethan's right.

I steady myself against a bookshelf, both of my hands against a wooden shelf with the letter *S* emblazoned on them in Courier, my eyes straying over the titles, from the tops of the shelves to the books at the very bottom, where the most neglected books live

SUCH A GOOD GIRL

simply by the disadvantage of being written by an author with an unlucky last name. I'm somewhere in fiction, and I've been strolling through the library, through the rows of computers in the labs, through the last of the paper periodicals, waiting for the students lolling about during their passing period to clear out.

Those students don't care if they're in trouble. They expect to be—they wait around on purpose, drawing out the time slowly, languidly. They know they're up to something and everyone else knows it too, and they're in the library to sop up as much time as possible away from class until they get in enough measurable trouble to have to return.

It's how they live: How much trouble is permissible? How much before it's too much and affects them in some meaningful way?

But they, the typical troublemakers, could never get away with what I'm about to do.

In the corner of the library, there is a nondescript wooden door that the faculty enter through and exit from throughout the day. If I simply stood near the door and peered inside, I wouldn't see much—mainly a white hall with two faculty bathrooms. Most of the students don't even know what it is. The teachers keep it quiet. It's better that way.

But I know what lies past the hallway.

I know a lot of things.

If one would walk through the wooden door and down the hall past the two faculty bathrooms, there would be yet another door, this one with a little brown placard that reads two simple, powerful words:

TEACHERS' LOUNGE.

57

I adjust my backpack on my shoulders.

A library aide pushes a metal cart past me through the aisles, one wheel squeaking as she presses lonely books into gaps onto their shelves. She catches sight of me and smiles, hesitantly, as if she can sense I'm not a typical loiterer, and then pushes the cart on, the wheel complaining in evenly timed little bursts.

She wouldn't stop me.

I can do this. I can break rules too.

My heart thunders strangely and my palms feel cold. I don't do things like this.

But I will.

I start moving toward the small door, my steps measured, even. I don't pause for even a second—I push through it and disappear into the white hallway, where I immediately run into Mrs. Carter-Smithy, a freshman English teacher, a pile of student notebooks in her arms.

"Riley!" she says, smiling at me.

"Good afternoon," I say smoothly, no trace of a quiver in my voice. Normal Riley would offer to help her with her notebooks and make conversation about her classes this year, but today I am not normal Riley.

And Mrs. Carter-Smithy doesn't ask what I'm doing.

She doesn't even pause.

She leaves the hallway and walks back into the library, like there would be a perfectly good reason why Riley Elizabeth Stone is hanging out in the hallway outside the teachers' lounge, where students are definitely not allowed.

SUCH A GOOD GIRL

And there is.

I walk down the hallway, past the two faculty bathrooms and the faculty water fountain that looks like it has never been used (or at least, never had chewing gum stuck to the spout).

And then, I enter the teachers' lounge.

And it is *glorious*.

When the library was redone, apparently they spared no expense when they renovated the teachers' lounge. Art—good stuff, too, not just stuff that looks like it's been lifted from the walls of a Motel 6—decorates the walls in polished wooden frames. There are pudgy leather chairs squatting comfortably around a small fireplace, a couple of mod tables with cute little stools, and best of all, free food.

On a counter in the kitchenette area, a yellow bowl of fresh fruit sits next to an array of granola bars and packs of Skittles and M&M's. A refrigerator squats in the corner with a sign on it that says FREE DRINKS—LIMIT ONE PER DAY.

The teachers have it so much better than I *ever* thought.

They barely look at me as I walk in.

Mr. Wellingsby, the art teacher, is lounging in one of the chairs, legs up over an arm, staring bemusedly out the window, his fingers in a small bag of chips. Mr. Codsworth and Ms. Sidmore, both middle-age math teachers (unmarried, rumored to be dating), are deep in conversation at a table. And then there's Mrs. Garder, the geography teacher, who is arguing with someone on her cell phone.

They all sort of glance at me, but no one bothers to even say anything.

I take a deep breath.

59

If I look like I belong, then I definitely belong.

I cross the teachers' lounge, threading my way through the little tables, and then open the fridge, which is filled with sodas and juices and waters and lunches labeled with first names I never bothered knowing.

I grab a sparkling water and shut the refrigerator. Mr. Wellingsby looks at me quizzically, so I smile.

He smiles back, disarmed, and goes back to his window-gazing.

Someone robbing a bank wouldn't smile, after all.

And then I walk out, not bothering to hide the Pellegrino in my hand. I let the door close softly behind me.

And no one says anything.

No one stops me.

No one runs out of the teachers' lounge, asking me what I'm up to or why I've taken something.

I blink slowly, turning back to look at the door.

At the little wooden placard.

TEACHERS' LOUNGE.

I. Did. It.

I rush into the bathroom, blood singing in my veins, and lean forward, my hands resting on either side of the white sink, trying not to look at the hair trapped in the drain.

I stare in the mirror.

I, Riley Elizabeth Stone, just stole something from the teachers' lounge.

While being late to class.

In front of actual teachers.

SUCH A GOOD GIRL

And no one bothered to stop me because, well, I'm me.

I smile at myself in the mirror. Maybe Ethan's right. And maybe—maybe there's something more to this whole thing.

Maybe being a Goody Two-shoes is the best cover ever for having a little fun.

What is it like to get in trouble, anyway?

And suddenly, in an odd way, I'm excited.

I walk down the empty hallway, my heels clattering on the tiles, and it feels . . . oddly normal, except that usually I have a pass in my hand, a piece of paper proclaiming me exempt from rules. I open the door of the Shakespeare classroom and step inside, counting my breaths. One second in, one second out.

The Shakespeare oil painting hanging on the opposite wall stares at me accusingly.

"Oh! Riley! I thought maybe you were out today."

"Nope, sorry, Mrs. Hamilton." I give her my specially formulated teacher smile, with a lot of teeth, and she returns it.

And I sit down.

Just like normal.

And she goes on teaching.

Just like normal.

Like I'm not late. Like I haven't just been playing a thief in the teachers' lounge.

"Riley? Would you please read for Macbeth today?" asks Mrs. Hamilton.

This makes me doubly sure she's not mad. I love reading for Macbeth. It's my favorite. And I love Mrs. Hamilton because she

61

will let girls read big parts—she's not one of those teachers who forces girls to read only the female parts and vice versa.

I smile to myself between lines.

It's almost like being good is the perfect alibi for being bad. I read my lines on autopilot, and I think about my next class. PE.

I actually like PE. And I have it with Kolbie and Neta, which means it's a chance to hang out with my buddies. And today we're supposed to just jog around the indoor track, which means it'll be pretty easy overall. Mr. Gladstone, the PE teacher, doesn't really care if you're giving a million percent as long as you're moving around a little bit and he doesn't have to do sex talks more than twice a year.

But I don't really want to change into my crappy gym uniform today, and I'm pretty sure I left my sports bra in the trunk of my car. Besides, Neta, Kolbie, and I were going to meet at Annie Up's, a cute little coffee shop and café a few steps off campus, for lunch. Would it be so bad if I just went there a little early?

So when the bell rings at the end of Shakespeare, I tuck *Macbeth* into my bag . . . but instead of going to gym, I slip out the side door next to the weight room and head over to Annie Up's, where I snag a table next to the window and order myself a caramel latte. I put my sunglasses on and pull a long, dark pink ribbon out of my backpack, which I weave into my hair in a messy ponytail in lieu of my normal straight style. For just a few minutes, I allow myself to feel very special and sort of grown-up.

Ethan would be proud of me.

My phone buzzes.

It's the group messaging thread with Neta and Kolbie.

62

SUCH A GOOD GIRL

From Neta: WHERE ARE YOU??? ARE YOU SICK OR WHAT?

I smile. I should have texted them, really. Of course they'd think that something was wrong. I sip my drink.

Skipped. At Annie Up's. Will you two hurry? I'm starving.

Kolbie texts me back. Are you insane?!?! Can you put Riley on the phone pls?? Seriously???

I giggle, thinking of them running around the track with their phones out. They're probably cursing.

See you two at lunch. Cover if Mr. Gladstone asks about me.

Neta: SERIOUSLY GIRL ARE YOU KIDNAPPED OR WHAT

I push my sunglasses up and send them a picture of myself with my latte so they're positive that I am not being held hostage or being forced to skip gym by hostile means. It would ruin my day if my two best friends put out some sort of Amber Alert on me. Then I might actually get in trouble for skipping.

Kolbie: ????? WHAT THE ????????

I text them back. Is there anything happening this weekend? This town is boring. Can we go to a party?

I finish my latte, feeling sort of—smug. A waitress brings me the lunch menu, and I order my salad early and a piece of Oreo cheesecake for dessert. I also order Kolbie and Neta's standbys: a grilled cheese, tomato soup, and lemonade for Kolbie, and a grilled chicken panini, french fries, and a strawberry smoothie for Neta.

Twenty minutes later, my friends burst in, and Neta's normally smooth hair is still in a lumpy gym ponytail. Kolbie is her normal perfect self. They both sit down at the table with me, and Kolbie looks super pissed.

63

"What the hell was that, Riley?" she asks. "Do you want to explain?"

I lift a shoulder, the same way I did at Ethan's. "Didn't feel like getting into gym clothes. Was Gladstone pissed?"

Neta heaves a theatrical sigh. "No. He said he thought you had some extra work in the library or something and marked you like you were *there*. But seriously. Is something wrong? And what are you doing with your hair?"

"Nothing's wrong." I see the waitress come out of the kitchen with our plates. "Oh, and I ordered your food for you so you don't have to eat so fast to get to class. Hope you don't mind."

Kolbie's face softens slightly when she sees her order. "Thanks. But you need to talk to us, Riley. We were *worried*. Like, legit, Neta was about to call 911. No joke, she had it typed into her phone and everything."

"I'm sorry," I say, knowing they want me to feel bad. I stir the ice in my drink with my straw. "I should have told you before. It was a split-second decision, though."

"But *why*? I just don't get you, Riley," Neta says. "One day you're having a total meltdown about losing a point on a test and the next day you're risking detention. What's going on?" Her lips are pinched with concern.

"I'm just tired of being me all the time. I wanted to do something—different." I sigh. I can't explain it to them. It doesn't make sense unless you've been . . . *me*.

"Well," Kolbie says slowly, "were you serious about the party this weekend?"

I kick my feet up on the chair across from me and shave off little

SUCH A GOOD GIRL

bits of Oreo cheesecake with my fork. "If you guys will take me."

"Are you sure you didn't mean a fund-raiser? Or, like, some sort of event where you're, like, saving malnourished owls or feeding hungry children or something?" Neta asks.

I shake my head. She's kidding, but not really. I'm sort of known for fund-raisers and social events where I order clothes from, like, Rent the Runway and then accept awards on behalf of high school kids who care or something while pretending to be a teenage Oscar nominee.

But not this time. I want to go out.

And I'm going to drink.

Maybe even a beer.

Neta hits me playfully in the arm with the back of her hand. "Seriously, Ri? Have we or have we not been begging you to party with us since we were in, like, eighth grade?"

I let myself smile, just a little bit. "Maybe."

Neta grabs her strawberry smoothie and her phone. "It's so on this weekend. You have no idea. Carlos is having a pool party in the hills, which is going to be nice. His parents have an indoor pool, you know. Or we could go to the south side to Alice's, which is more of a chill hang. Or we could just go old school and drive around and we see what we run into."

"I'm in."

"Which one?" Neta asks.

I smile evilly. "All of them."

65

SEVEN
Almost

"Jell-O shots for the ladies?" Mario Anders asks, holding a silver pizza tray of multicolored Dixie cups. "I have cherry, lemon, grape, and I think maybe a couple of strawberries left, but you're going to have to act fast."

"Sure!" Neta squeals, taking a lemon. She grabs a strawberry and a grape, and hands the red one to me. "Only if you're comfortable," she assures me, and I sniff it tentatively.

We're all crammed on a fat leather couch on the second floor of a huge mansion up in the hills, and Neta and Kolbie seem like they're having an *amazing* time because they're on their third drinks already. The music is loud enough that the walls seem to be throbbing with it, and I am fairly certain the playlist has been lifted

SUCH A GOOD GIRL

from the seventies or something because I have recognized only one song and that's because I heard it in a movie.

Kolbie and Neta are laughing and smiling at everyone, our legs are sweating and sticking to the couch, and I'm trying to imitate them and not think about how sweaty my butt is going to look when I stand up, or if I'm actually going to have something to contribute to a conversation at some point, or whether this is what they talk about every Monday in study hall when they talk about *fun* and what happened over the weekend and how I *totally missed out again.*

Someone brought in cheesy disco lights, and they're flashing around at the top of the main staircase in time with the beat, and there is a stocky blond boy in a cutoff T-shirt doing strange dance moves on the marble foyer downstairs.

It's not going well for him so far.

I try not to look out the window for the eightieth time that evening. The cops are not here. In fact, there are no cops. If the cops were going to come here, they would not even be here to bust anyone. Carlos Rodriguez's family is wealthy and well regarded, so no one would ever *dare* call the cops on a party at their house. In fact, if the cops were here, it would probably be to keep people from entering the party. That's how exclusive these parties are, in fact.

At least, that's what Kolbie told me. Apparently, Kolbie and Neta have been to a million of Carlos's parties, and it's always pretty safe and a lot of *fun.* And that's why they decided to ease me in with a fancy Rodriguez party before, like, taking me to a gas station to illegally buy forties or something.

"Do you know how to do a Jell-O shot?" Kolbie yells into my

67

ear, grabbing the purple shot. I can barely hear her, and she's right next to me.

"I don't have a spoon!" I yell back. I chance another look out the window, but I don't see any flashing lights. I glance around. They didn't hand out any plastic silverware, which seems like common sense, honestly.

"You have to use your finger to loosen it up," Neta says, running her finger around the edge of the cup. "And then you just tip it back." She lets all of the Jell-O fall into her mouth and swallows it. "Yum. And you can't even, like, taste the vodka. It's so good, Riley."

Kolbie just squeezes the Dixie cup into her mouth, which looks a little less neat, so I decide to go Neta's route. It's actually not bad. It's fruity and sweet and slides down my throat easily, but leaves just a slight bitter aftertaste on the back of my tongue. It's better than the wheaty beer I've been nursing for the past hour and a half.

"Are you buzzing?" Kolbie asks me. "Do you want anything else?"

"Um, no thanks," I say. I don't think I like drinking much, and honestly, I don't feel a thing.

"The more you drink, the less you'll worry about getting caught," Kolbie says. "I know that's terrible real-world advice, but it's actually true." She tosses her cup at some guy walking by with a huge garbage bag, who tries to catch it, but it bounces off onto the wood floor.

Neta pulls on my arm. "It's too hot on this couch. Let's go talk to more people! We can see if there are any cute guys here from Bellview, okay? Oh!" She releases me for a second and digs in her

68

SUCH A GOOD GIRL

wristlet, producing a bright pink tube of lip gloss. "Try this on, okay? I think you need some."

I stare at it for a second. It's way too bright for me. I know it. But this whole party isn't me. The point of the night isn't me. So I unscrew the top of the lip gloss and dab a little onto my lips to appease her. "Right back, Kolbie!" Neta says, and drags me away to a group of guys that she just dives right into, introducing me to Zayne and Jordan and Benn (with two *N*'s, he tells us, which is apparently way better than a Ben with just one.).

"I've heard about you," Zayne says, taking my hand and holding it for just a second too long. "You're the one who never comes out."

Wow. Even other schools know I'm a shut-in goody-goody. Still, I rather like Zayne. He has a wide smile with even teeth. His hair is dark and curly and he's just tall enough.

"Don't I?" I ask Zayne. "Then what am I doing here?"

Zayne smiles. "Surprising me. That means something."

"Enlighten me, Zayne. What does it all mean?"

"You're about to be my . . . beer pong partner. Right?"

"Sure, but there are conditions. Two, to be exact."

"Anything." Zayne grins, anticipating my response.

I hold up one finger. "Only if you teach me how to play." I smile at him as I take another drink of my warm beer. What am I getting myself into? I pop up a second finger. "And only if we play against Neta and her partner of choice."

Neta slides her arm around Benn with two *N*'s. "You better be good at beer pong."

He finishes his beer. "I've never lost . . . tonight."

"You haven't played tonight!" she accuses, and they're laughing together and he's looking down at her like she's everything and she's looking up at him like . . . well, like he's a beer pong partner she's going to have to peel off later.

Zayne leads us downstairs, to a room near the pool where a Ping-Pong table has been set up with several Solo cups filled halfway with beer. He explains the rules—if the other team gets a Ping-Pong ball in your set of cups, you have to drink. It's basically a game that would be super lame if beer weren't involved. I turn to Zayne. "We have a problem," I whisper.

"What?" He looks at me, alarmed.

I grin at him and pull at the neck of his shirt. "I hate beer. So if we lose—"

"I'm stuck drinking most of it," he finishes, and laughs. "Some partnership this is!"

"You chose me!" I accuse. "So this is totally on you."

"I don't regret it yet."

Neta winks at me from across the table, and I resist rolling my eyes. It's like they think I don't know how to flirt. It's not like it's hard. You just have to appeal to the three basic drunken categories for party boys:

1. Beer

2. Sports (of some kind)

3. Sex

Boom. Flirting. Done.

It's not rocket science. It's not even a challenge. And

SUCH A GOOD GIRL

honestly . . . it's a little boring. Is this how all parties are? Slightly bitter shots with Ping-Pong balls in skunky beer?

Is this what Ethan wanted me to throw everything away for? Was this a domino even worth knocking over?

"Your throw," Zayne says, handing me a beer-soaked Ping-Pong ball. This is definitely not sanitary. "Make it count, Stone."

"Give me space, Zayne." I move him out of the way with my hip, which he seems to like, and line up my shot. I close one eye, and across the table, Benn and Neta jeer at me. Neta sticks out her tongue, and I laugh, but I don't lose my focus. This is Riley time. This is Zen and the Art of Beer Pong.

I toss the Ping-Pong ball.

It bounces off the first cup and lands in the second.

"Does that count?" I ask Zayne.

Zayne grabs my hand and forces a high five on me. "Hell yeah, it counts. Chug it, B team!" he shouts across the table.

Neta makes a pouty face and pulls the Ping-Pong ball out of the cup. She winks at me, takes a tiny sip, and then hands the rest of the cup to her partner, who downs it, two rivulets of beer leaking out over both of his stubbly cheeks. "Woo!" he says, wiping off his face with the back of his hand. "I feel good!"

"We get to shoot again!" Zayne says, grabbing another ball. "Go, Stone!"

I line up again, and this time the ball goes long, hitting Benn in the shirt. "Damn!" I say, but Zayne pats me on the small of my back. His hand lingers for a millisecond.

"Don't worry," he says. "We got 'em the next time. Now we have to distract them." He shouts across the table, and I join him, feeling stupid. Suddenly, I want to leave.

But this is a *party*. This is what I've gotten myself into.

They miss.

Our go.

This is what people my age *do*. Right?

I sigh. I watch Zayne toss the ball. It makes it into one of their cups, and I cheer and we high-five again, and then I miss and so the ball goes to the other team. This time Zayne tells me I have to drink, and so I down as much as I can from the Solo cup and then hand the beer off to him to finish, feeling a little queasy and strange, like maybe my vision isn't following quite right when I turn my head and my smile isn't matching up on my mouth the way it should be.

The Ping-Pong ball changes hands again.

How lame would it be if I used hand sanitizer on it? Would that make the beer taste better, or worse? Or would anyone even notice?

Maybe Kolbie has it right with her college boyfriend. College parties have to be better than this, right? They have to be more fun. More . . . sophisticated. More substantial.

Maybe there's talking. Like real talking, not just lame flirting over beer-soaked balls.

Or maybe it's just more of the same.

I feel a hand on my shoulder, and I turn. It's Kolbie. "How's it going, Ri? How much beer have you downed?"

I smile at her. "A cup. Or something."

SUCH A GOOD GIRL

She frowns at me. "Are you buzzing? You don't seem like you're buzzing."

I think I am, if this counts as buzzing. Beyond the eye thing, I have this strange warmth inside me, and I feel like I'm underwater, but just under the surface, where things are just a touch slower. But I'm just a little drunk, and somehow it's not the happy, fun place where everyone else seems to be.

"I'm good," I tell her, and she slings an arm around my shoulder.

"I think maybe I should take my friend's place here," she tells them. "So she can run to the bathroom. She'll be right back. Won't you, Ri?" She puts her hands on my shoulders and looks in my eyes, telling me in friend code to take as much time away from the stupid game as I need.

I tell her back in friend language that I'm grateful, and turn to Zayne. "Be right back. Don't screw it up, okay? We have a lot riding on this game."

It's strange how it all comes so easily to me. The words, with no feeling to back them up.

He fist-bumps me. "We've got this in the cup."

I smile widely at his lame joke and escape in the general direction of a bathroom. The first two I find are locked, but I finally find a small one, just off the pool, that's more of a changing room than anything else. I flick on the light, but then after I've closed the door, I flick it off and slide down to the floor and savor being alone, just for a second.

I want to go home. I want to be at home, in my room, on my bed. Alone. These people who are like me on the outside are not

73

my people. It's not like there's anything wrong with them. Tonight I know the truth: there is something wrong with me.

I lean my head back against the door and close my eyes, but someone knocks.

"Ri? You in there?"

Kolbie.

I reach up and turn the lock on the door.

"What are you doing in here in the dark?" She walks in and flicks on the light. "Are you okay?"

I try to smile. "Yeah. Sorry. I just needed a minute. These guys—I don't know." I flutter my hand.

Kolbie looks at me. "Yeah. I get it. I feel that way too. I told your boy Zayne to take my turn and came to find you."

I sigh, and she sinks down on the floor next to me, and I lean my head on her chest. "These are not my people."

"No, they aren't. But that's okay." She pauses, and pretend silence fills the room, but outside, the music from the party pounds, the bass so thick and heavy I can feel it through the floor. "Maybe we shouldn't be pushing you to be with someone. Or maybe you just need someone older. I'm just . . . I'm sorry if we put too much pressure on you. We didn't mean anything, you know?"

I nod. "I know."

She gets me.

But then I wonder . . . is she talking about someone in particular? Someone we both know?

No.

That's impossible.

SUCH A GOOD GIRL

Of course not.

"Do you want to go home?" she asks.

I nod. My head is starting to spin in a fuzzy, strange way, and my stomach feels odd and too full. I don't feel sick, but I am starting to feel a little out of control.

And what if the cops really did show up?

All my dominoes would really be knocked down then. That would sure show Ethan for trying to make me an actual teenager.

"Come on, Ri." She pushes herself off the floor, then reaches down and grabs my hand to help me up. "I think this is enough party for one night."

"You're a good friend," I tell her, leaning on her shoulder a little bit. She stumbles, then rights herself, slinging my arm around her waist.

She pauses. "Don't forget all the nights you've picked me up off the floor and held my hair and let me sneak into your house when I'm late for my curfew." She winces. "Actually, *do* forget them, please."

I smile and squeeze her a little. "I'm here for you, Kolbs." The words are slippery in my mouth.

She smiles back. "I know you are, Riley."

EIGHT
Bookstore

There is something about bookstores.

Something better about bookstores than parties or movies or pictures. There's something hidden in books; lives and secrets and whispers and little bits of truth you could never guess at, even if you'd known the author her entire life and then read the book and asked her all about it. I think there are little bits of truth in books that are probably never discovered, even by the people who write them.

And also I like to read.

Smart girl problems.

It is Saturday afternoon, and I woke up with a little bit of a headache. I poured myself a glass of filtered water and took two

SUCH A GOOD GIRL

Tylenol before wrapping up in a big, loose henley and a gauzy lavender scarf and twisting my hair into a long golden braid. I walked to my favorite bookstore: a small one in South York Village called Pockets, where people laze around outside with croissants on little tables and drink tea in clay mugs with milk and sugar.

Inside, the rows are all hunched very closely together, and the shelves are old and splintering under the weight of the books, often stacked two high and three deep. They smell wonderful, like aged glue and ancient paper, and I draw slow breaths as I walk in, savoring the quiet scent that is only noticeable to the type of people who truly love it there.

This is a place that I could not take Kolbie and Neta and have them understand it quite the way I understand it. It's not that they don't like books; they do. They're both quite intelligent. It's just that this store is something to me, and I'm something to it, and I'm not entirely excited to share it with my friends, who might not find the peeling wallpaper appealing, or like the fact that the tap in the bathroom only runs cold.

I walk through the poetry section, and I pull out a secondhand copy of *Burning in Water, Drowning in Flame*, when I hear the voice. The unmistakable voice.

"Darling, what do you want?"

"I don't know. Do they have magazines here?" She pouts, and I imagine her sticking out her lower lip just slightly.

"Maybe old ones. I don't know. Don't you want a novel or something?"

I peek away from my Bukowski poems, and there they are: Alex

77

Belrose and his beautiful wife, Jacqueline, on the other end of the row. Mr. Belrose has a lanky arm around his spouse, who is lithe and fair and lovely, like she's stepped out of the pages of French *Vogue* after being artfully arranged by a fashion photographer. I heard Alex met her while he was studying abroad in France. She's American, of course, and so is he, but apparently they had this great, wild love story that sounds, naturally, like something that never actually happened. She's long-limbed and gorgeous and has a nose like a lost pink button. Her clothes hang on her like wings on a grand sort of bird; they're jewel-toned and spread out around her like she's some sort of queen.

She's no ordinary woman. At least, that's what people say.

I look down at my book of poems, running my finger along the page even though I've stopped reading the words some time ago. I tuck myself farther back, wishing I could disappear. I don't want to talk to Jacqueline. Don't want to have to be measured next to her. I feel small and lesser and strange, and I wish neither of them were here and this little bookstore were still mine, just mine, and I didn't have to worry about interlopers, even pretty ones I've dreamed about running into.

I rearrange my scarf so it's draped around my arms and covering my back and turn away from the storefront so no one can see me, when someone taps on my shoulder.

"Hello."

I turn around so quickly I almost lose my balance. I stumble a little. It's Mr. Belrose.

"Oh. Hey."

SUCH A GOOD GIRL

He grins. "I'm sorry. Did I scare you? Am I not allowed to talk to you outside of school hours?"

I look to the left and the right, like I'm scouting for someone. "Strictly against policy," I whisper. "I actually didn't know they let teachers out of the school. I thought they lived there. Had to take showers in the sinks and all that."

He nods solemnly. "You know our secrets, then. But they do let us out, for two hours each weekend, to give the appearance of being real people."

I snap my fingers. "It almost worked."

He chuckles. "Damn it." Mr. Belrose's eyes drop to my hands, and he lifts the poetry book from them. "Bukowski, hmm?"

"Yes," I say. "He's my favorite poet."

"He's a bit dark for my sunshiny-est student," Mr. Belrose says.

"Perhaps there's more to me than meets the eye," I say, then immediately hate myself. *Did I really just say that? To a* teacher*? Am I stupid?*

"That," Mr. Belrose says, "I'm not surprised about. But I've never been much of a poetry fan, unless it's classic and French. I prefer a good novel in your cheap American tongue." He smiles, and runs his fingers over the spines of the books on the shelves fondly. "I come here on the weekends often. I've found a lot of my favorites in this very store."

"Really?" I fold my arms over my chest.

He glances back at me. "You don't have to sound so surprised. Take, for example, Stephen King." He plucks a copy of *The Shining* off the shelf. "I love a good horror novel as much as the next

79

person." He slides it back with reverence. "Or maybe Hemingway. I love a sharply written book, you know? *The Old Man and the Sea* is my absolute favorite. But you . . . you're different. I can tell. Dark stuff. Stuff that you can't find in the high school library. Beyond a typical horror."

"There's other stuff too," I protest. "I love Jane Austen as much as the next girl. And I love romance novels. And I enjoy Shakespeare." I turn a corner and flick a copy of *The Complete Works of William Shakespeare* with my index finger and thumb, completely mis-shelved. "I love young-adult novels and picture books and anything I can read with chocolate-chip cookies and mint tea." I run my hands over the spines, just like he did, my fingers picking up particles of dust.

"Ah." He clasps his hands behind his back.

"Ah?" I ask. "What does 'Ah,' mean, then?"

"Can I make a suggestion?"

"Do I have a choice?"

I feel dangerous, flirting with him with Jacqueline so close by. I am warm suddenly, so I take my scarf off and tuck it hastily in my bag.

"Always." He just looks at me, no trace of a smile around his lips, his green eyes intense.

"Darling? Where are you?"

The lilt of the voice is unmistakable.

Unwillingly, my heart sinks a little.

Mr. Belrose turns. "Right here, Jackie." He whips back to me, and he presses a book into my hands urgently, and I realize I don't

SUCH A GOOD GIRL

know if he's had it this whole time or if he's just pulled it from a shelf. "Read this," he says. "It'll do you good. And tell me what you think. Tell me what it makes you feel."

I find myself drawing the book in to my stomach and holding it tightly. Mr. Belrose walks toward the end of the aisle and waves at his wife. She comes toward him, a stack of magazines, which look like *People* and *Us Weekly* and *OK!*, balanced on her arm.

"Are you ready? I'm so bored." Her voice is a high-pitched whine, and I hate her a little then, for being bored in my perfect little bookstore and ruining everything.

"Sure," Mr. Belrose says. "Do you want all of those?"

"I'm bored," she insists again by way of answer. She thrusts the magazines at him, and he takes them under his arm.

"Okay." Mr. Belrose turns to me and lifts his hand. "Good-bye, Riley. I'll see you in class. Enjoy your books, okay?"

I wave at him, feeling a pang somewhere between my stomach and chest.

It isn't until I've paid the man at the cash register and I'm back at my house that I realize that somewhere along the way I've lost my pretty scarf.

It must have fallen out of my bag.

81

NINE
Untruths

School buses are genuinely the worst. I don't know what it is, but there's something about being underage that makes the bus designers say, *Okay, let's literally forgo every creature comfort in a traditional vehicle and just go with the absolute bare minimum. Like, let's just slap gray vinyl seats (no seat belts needed) into a metal shell and put a bunch of children on it and call it good. And if the engine sounds like it might explode at any possible moment, that's fine, it's not like the cargo is important in any way.*

Meanwhile other buses have plush seats and air-conditioning, heat that works without making the engine whine, and televisions.

"I always get my best sleep on a school bus," Neta says, yawning and leaning her head on my shoulder. "I love these seats. It's like

SUCH A GOOD GIRL

BO has permanently worked its way into the material. It's so sooth-ing." She takes a deep breath and coughs.

I fake-gag. "You're so gross."

"Don't be mad at me because I'm honest." She snuggles in deeper against my shoulder. "I'm just gonna sleep here, mkay? These gross buses are the best for sleeping."

She's right. There's something about the rhythm of a bus that's relaxing . . . maybe the lack of shocks as it bumbles over the road . . . or maybe it's, like, carbon monoxide leaking in and slowly poisoning us. It's possible.

I yawn, but I resist sleep. We're on the way to our mock trial meet. I'm playing a witness today: a psychiatrist who has to attest to the sanity of the plaintiff. I run over my notes for the meet, then I glance over at Neta, whose eyes are closed. She's breathing softly through her mouth. I lean over very slowly and feel around in my bag for something . . . one specific book, used, with a cloth bind-ing. With one hand, I slide it up my leg and into my lap.

It's the book that Mr. Belrose chose for me in the store. It's the one he pressed into my hands and told me to read. It's called *L'Amant.*

The Lover.

And it means something.

The whole book is in French, of course, so I'm working my way through it, slowly, carefully, looking up words on my phone and rereading passages and pages, but there is a message for me in it, I am sure.

There has to be.

83

L'Amant is the story of a young girl who meets a twenty-seven-year-old businessman. The girl is even younger than me. The man is just a year older than Mr. Belrose. I work through the pages painstakingly.

"What's that?"

Neta's awake.

I feel my face color. "Um, nothing." I let my hair swing down in front of my cheek, which is becoming a defense mechanism.

"Doesn't look like nothing." She rubs her eyes and sits up. "Where did you get it?"

"School." The lie comes easily, like I've had it lying in wait this whole time. "Just schoolwork." I say a silent prayer of thanks that neither Neta or Kolbie take French . . . and hopefully don't understand any of it, either. Both of them would have signed up for it had they not already been in advanced Spanish classes.

"Oh. Boring. I thought it would be, like, a sexy book, but you're reading homework?" She sighs. "Leave it to you to get all hot and bothered about an assignment. Give it a break, Ri. We practically have the day off."

"You could be prepping for your part," I remind her.

She pulls her hood up and yanks the strings on her jacket to bring it tighter around her face. "You are missing out on quality school bus sleep time," she points out. "You really need to put away your books and chill out for one second. What happened to rule-breaking Riley from the weekend who was, like, 'yay alcohol, let's take off all our clothes and get arrested'?"

I cock my head and rest my chin on my wrist, pretending to

SUCH A GOOD GIRL

think. "You're so right. Thanks for providing that direct quote. Except you left out all the stuff about the drugs that I think I yelled from a plane before I jumped out of it with a homemade parachute."

"I edited out the swear words." Neta giggles. She puts on a pair of black sunglasses and tilts her head back onto the top of the seat. "Now stop waking me up with your smart-people stuff."

I sigh and slip the book back into my backpack between my Shakespeare homework and a copy of *The Sun Also Rises*. I don't want anyone in my French class to catch me reading it either. They might actually translate the title correctly . . . and then I'd have to lie even better.

Everyone knows the best lies are the least complicated.

Besides, there's a part of me that wants to read the book alone, maybe when I'm about to go to sleep. There's something about it that feels . . . personal. Like maybe someone is whispering in my ear, telling me a secret that's meant to be heard only when no one else is around and I'm tucked in bed, under my covers, listening to the house breathing while everyone else is asleep.

Still, why wouldn't I tell Neta that Mr. Belrose gave me the book? She'd love knowing that I ran into him and his beautiful wife in the bookstore. There isn't really anything to hide with my French teacher. Everyone else has a crush on him, after all. Is it so odd that his star pupil does too? Neta and Kolbie would be terribly jealous and I'd get tell them everything he said to me. And it would be sort of nice to tell them. Tell *someone*, at least. Would it really be so horrible to admit it? Besides, it's not as if there's something going on.

Is there?

I shiver suddenly and look out the window, at the passing trees and fields. There isn't. It's just a book that happens to be published in French, and I happened to be at the used bookstore at the exact same time as Belrose and his wife. I rest my forehead against the glass, and Neta snores softly beside me. I feel my phone buzz in my pocket and pull it out to check my e-mails. There's a few new ones . . . something from the shoe store at the mall, a 20 percent off coupon to Abercrombie this weekend, and . . . another e-mail.

Something unopened from an address I've not received a message from before. At least, not that I can remember.

And I would remember.

Because it's an address I can identify.

An e-mail that contains the names Alex and Belrose.

The e-mail itself contains one word:

Enjoying?

My veins flood with something like ice and then with a liquid burst of heat and then ice again. I know who it is without asking. I know immediately.

Suddenly, and oddly, I almost want to put my phone down. I want to delete the message and drop the phone and pretend the message never came to me at all, and that a teacher is not reaching out to his student about a rather naughty French book he gave her at her favorite bookstore and everything is normal, just very normal and fine, quite fine, thank you.

But I can't do that.

Very much so. Thanks for the recommendation. My finger hovers

SUCH A GOOD GIRL

over the send button for almost thirty seconds, but then I touch it and the e-mail is gone.

And almost as quickly, one comes back.

It's a favorite of mine.

My heart pounds. I glance at Neta and angle myself away from her, drawing my knees up on the seat to put a barrier between us, so I have a small private space to send messages.

Any particular reason why? I ask.

Read it, and I think you'll know.

I am.

Good girl.

The last e-mail startles me. *Good girl?* The verbiage is highly condescending and too personal all at once, and I'm not sure how to respond. Because he's right. I am just a good girl.

I stare at my phone, but he doesn't send any more e-mails. I can't think of anything else to say, and I feel like there is a cement mixer in my stomach tossing around feelings like sick and happy and excited and horrible. I lean my head against the window and watch the blur of the asphalt through the glass.

Things to Know About Riley Stone:

- When Riley was ten, she started a fund-raiser to collect warm socks for the homeless. She engaged twelve schools and collected more than 1,500 pairs of socks for local shelters.
- Riley kept one super-cute purple pair for herself because hey, no one said ten-year-olds were perfect.
- At age twelve, Riley won the opportunity to make a speech at the local chapter of a veterans' organization. She spoke about what their service meant to her and her great-grandfather, who served in Vietnam. Riley received a standing ovation, and to date, the video has received 130,000 YouTube hits, which unfortunately is not quite viral by Riley standards.
- When Riley was in middle school, she set national records for most Girl Scout cookies sold by selling her wares outside of frat houses notorious for partying.
- At age seven, Riley, ever the type A, began to enter behavioral therapy because her parents worried about her taking on too much. Her therapists and psychiatrists agreed it was a good choice for a girl with her tendencies, but Mr. and Mrs. Stone were nervous about any social ramifications the therapy could have if Riley was ever found out, so she was never allowed to attend more than a few weeks of continual therapy at a time.

TEN
Secret

Good girl.

He's right.

He is.

That sums me up. Certainly, I was late to class. I skipped class. I drank beer and played games and went to a real party and did all the things that high school students are supposed to do for one stupid weekend, but that doesn't mean anything at all. It's not like it changed me in any real way.

I'm in the good-girl category. I live there. I am listed there firmly, my name printed, and a solid black checkmark next to it. My brother is still a bit lost, even though he's found Esther and he thinks he's in love, and we're all just stuck unless we do something drastic and wild that changes our hearts and tears up our souls a little bit.

Good girl.

I don't know why it bothers me so much, but it follows me. It tails me back to school. It follows me back into French class and sits curled on my shoulder and slides up my neck to whisper in my ear.

It's nothing, I'm nothing else.

Mr. Belrose doesn't look at me in any special way when he hands our tests back. He doesn't give me a special wink, or a specific smile. He treats me like he treats Thea . . . like someone holding on to something a bit distasteful, arm extended, away from the body. Like what you're holding is important enough that you can't drop it, but God forbid you let it near enough to actually *touch* you.

"Might I remind you all," Mr. Belrose says, "that essays are due today." He smiles at us like this is a special day, one we've all been waiting for.

About a month ago, he assigned us a monster essay. A huge one. Eight pages. Which would suck in any class, honestly.

Except that Belrose said it *all* had to be *en français*.

Which meant it was a *beast* of a homework assignment, and even the girls who were nursing huge crushes on Mr. Belrose were sort of grumbling about it because it was definitely not one of those things you could dash off the evening before in a Red Bull–infused rush of chemical energy.

Of course, I wrote mine on Julius Caesar conquering Gaul and had it done two weeks ago and made it *ten* pages long because

SUCH A GOOD GIRL

French history is really rich and interesting, and eight pages was just not enough to accurately cover the whole Roman takeover and how it was all about debt, but that's just me.

I pull my essay out of my folder and walk it up to Mr. Belrose's desk.

He is wearing glasses again today. Ones with thick black frames. They accentuate the deep green of his eyes, but I try not to notice. Deep green eyes are not my business.

He glances at me, and the corner of his mouth pulls up, just slightly. So slightly I hardly notice.

"*Merci*, Mademoiselle Stone."

His left hand moves to his side.

There is something gauzy and soft and lavender in his pocket.

Something—

Oh my God.

My scarf.

He watches as I notice. His deep green eyes—eyes that are suddenly my concern after all—fill with amusement.

His smile grows wider.

ELEVEN
Meanings

"How do you tell if a guy likes you?"

Neta and I are over at Kolbie's house, which is almost as nice as Carlos's. Her parents are super-overprotective and huge on family time, but they're usually cool about letting us hang out in the theater room in the basement.

Yeah. Her parents have a theater room. Her dad is some COO of an IT company, which means it's super-tricked-out, too, and there are speakers legitimately built into the floors.

"What do you mean?" Neta says. "And can you please pass me the Tiffany blue?"

I pass her the blue nail polish. We're all doing pedis while *Sixteen Candles* plays on the big screen. We're doing an old-

SUCH A GOOD GIRL

school movie night. We try to do these at least once a month. Some are, like, super-old-school, à la Audrey Hepburn, and some are, like, *10 Things I Hate About You*, which is about a five on the old-o-meter.

"Did you not see Zayne at the party?" Kolbie asks. "Or the way he was drooling all over you and laughing at, like, every half syllable that fell out of your mouth?" She grabs a white polish and tosses it to me. I'm trying to give my toes French tips. "Trying" being the operative word.

"I know like that." I grab the tiny polish and spread out a newspaper under my feet. "But, like, what about when it's more subtle?"

"Subtle like how?" Neta asks. She started to paint her toes, but now she's distracted and diving into popcorn. Her fingers are covered in butter.

Like when he has your scarf in his pocket. And when he keeps looking at you and touching it.

And when he's your teacher.

"Like, what if instead of trying to get you to sink balls into beer pong cups and tongue your neck, he's trying to just be nice to you or something?"

"RJ licked my neck on our first date," Neta says defensively.

"Look how great that turned out." Kolbie holds her foot out. "Do I like this pink? I think I like this pink better than the blue."

Neta throws a handful of popcorn at her.

"You're cleaning that up later," Kolbie warns. "My mom does not play."

"Stop dissing RJ, then."

95

"Stop defending someone who treated you like something he put down the garbage disposal."

Neta throws another handful of popcorn because she knows Kolbie is right, and Kolbie stands up. "Seriously?"

"Can we get back to the point?" I ask. I smudge a little bit of the white on the bottom of my toenail. Damn it.

"It would help if we knew who you were talking about," Neta points out. A piece of popcorn falls onto her chest, and she licks it up with her tongue.

Kolbie raises her eyebrows. "You are so classy I can't even deal."

Neta winks at her. "More where that came from."

I giggle. "Seriously, though. It's not a particular guy. I'm just talking about mature, non-drunk dudes who are maybe a little bit past their beer pong stage of life. Like, what's the protocol?"

Kolbie points at me with a pastel-pink-painted brush, and a glob of paint falls off onto the newspaper. "As the only one here who has experienced an actual healthy relationship, I think I should speak to this. First of all, he will find an excuse to touch you. And not in a creepy, grind-on-you-in-the-club kind of way. In a sweet way. Like, he'll touch your hand or something. Or pick an eyelash off your cheek. Or whatever."

"You're telling me," I say, "that Jamal picked an eyelash off your cheek? And that you didn't steal that from *The Notebook* or, like, *Insert Cheesy Date Movie Here*?"

"It was an actual occurrence. And he also started leaving stuff around so I'd have to return it. And I did the same. Like, I left an earring at his house once. And he left his iPod at mine."

SUCH A GOOD GIRL

I think of my scarf, and feel my face color slightly. Maybe it *does* mean something that he has it. And he's holding on to it. It *has* to.

I think of the way he looked at me when he touched it, and I feel *something* in my lower belly.

"It might take longer," Neta adds, "but he'll let you know. And that's when you know it's a good one. Like Jamal, right, Kolbie?"

Kolbie settles back into her recliner, satisfied with her toes. "Just like Jamal."

"You're lucky," Neta says. "I'm still on the neck-lickers."

"More serious topic," Kolbie says, pointing at the screen. "Can we talk about how messed up this movie is? Like, could we have a side of humor with this load of racism, please?"

"I was still stuck on the massive amount of date rape." Neta reaches for the remote. "Because that is just exactly the kind of message any girl wants to hear."

"Can we veto this movie?" I ask. "I'm over it."

We binge dating reality shows instead, and while they aren't, like, completely *free* of sexism or anything, they're at least a little better.

The next day in French class Mr. Belrose announces that the class will have a lot of homework coming up.

"Why?" whines Thea, pulling on her hair. "I thought you liked us, Mr. Belrose. I thought we were, like, your favorite class. And didn't we *just* finish the giant essay of doom?"

"Well, I'll have a lot of extra time in the next couple of weeks," he says. His eyes shift to me. "My wife's gone. She's visiting her mother."

97

He holds my gaze.

I hold his.

He wants me.

He does.

My heart wants to beat its way out of my chest.

Around me, the class *oohs*. "How will you occupy yourself while she is away, Monsieur Belrose?" Teri Von Millhouse asks. She leans forward on one hand and flutters her eyelashes.

"Catch up on my Netflix. And give you more homework." Belrose shakes his head, and I realize, suddenly, his hair is getting a little long. He reminds me of Alex. Not a teacher.

Just Alex. The guy that I used to know.

"I'll comfort you if you're lonely," Thea says, raising her hand.

"And that's my cue to tell you to turn to page two seventy-six in your textbook, guys, before things get any more awkward. Questions about my personal life will now result in additional homework. With reasonable exceptions." His eyes stray to me again, and I press my lips together to keep my feelings from showing on my face.

And I wonder what it would be like to kiss him.

I wonder if he would be tender.

Or if he would be aggressive.

The truth is I've never had a real kiss before. Well, at least not one that I count. I suppose there was Erick Canders in third grade during the school play. He slipped me tongue because he was coughing really hard.

Which I don't. Count it.

98

SUCH A GOOD GIRL

And I don't count the little ones I snuck on the playground when I was a little girl. The meaningless ones with boys behind trees, just to see what it was like.

A real kiss is different. A real kiss is with someone who means something.

And so I have never had a real kiss.

I watch Mr. Belrose as if there is nothing out of the ordinary. I take notes in deliberate, even handwriting, highlighting the most important sections in three different colors, and I write down my homework in my planner, which is a bit more than usual. And I don't stick around after class to talk to him, because Riley Stone has no reason to stick around to speak to her teacher, not when she has absolutely everything under control.

But when I get home that evening, I find the phone book in the cupboard underneath my parents' landline (they still have both because they are stuck in the last century and don't trust cell phones in disasters). I make a mental note of Belrose's address.

And then I grab my keys.

I know the street, I think—it's about twenty minutes away, not far from a park on the other side of town. It's not a wealthy part of town, but it's not like it's horrible, either. It's a typical lower-middle-class neighborhood: chain-link fences, well-tended gardens with chipped gnomes, kids playing basketball in their driveways.

I drum my feelings out on the steering wheel, but I can't process them. I'm not sure if my heart is working quite right. Or at all.

Am I misreading all the signals? What am I doing? Did he even want me? Am I completely nuts?

99

I park three blocks away, pull on one of Ethan's old Denver Broncos baseball caps, and slip out of my car. I stare in the direction of his house.

This is bad.

This isn't late-to-class bad. It's not drinking-beer bad. It's actually *bad* bad. There is no going back from this bad.

He's a teacher.

He's over eighteen.

He's *married*.

And I am a good girl.

My mind ticks back to his e-mail.

If I go over to his house, then that's gone. I'm not just stepping neatly out of the category I've been shuffled in—I'm basically blowing it up with a nuclear bomb.

I can't go back.

But my feet start moving in the direction of his house. The street is friendly enough. There are tons of trees—old ones, with thick trunks, casting the trees in shadows. I glance at the little homes as I walk by. None of them are very big. Some have children and dogs in the yard. Some are empty. Some of the lawns haven't been mowed in a while.

My footsteps feel too deliberate and strange, like I've never used my feet before. Am I walking casually? How does one walk casually?

I pull the baseball cap farther over my head and push my hair behind my ears.

Maybe I shouldn't have dressed so much like myself—all

SUCH A GOOD GIRL

straight edges and J.Crew and neat. Maybe I should have worn a disguise.

I feel oddly cold, and it's a nice day. My fingers and toes tingle strangely. What am I doing? Is this who I am now? Am I really interested in Alex Belrose?

Shouldn't I learn to be happy with Zaynes, drooling over me while I play beer pong? With Robs? Rob is so sweet. Why can't I be happy with Rob?

Rob and I even have a history. I mean, we never really dated, but we were friends. We sat next to each other in fourth grade, and for my birthday that year, he gave me a pink unicorn pencil with a white heart eraser. Every year since, he's slipped the same pink unicorn pencil into my locker on my birthday, and every year he smiles at me because we both know but we never say anything about it.

My chest hurts.

Because I can't.

Not with Rob.

He's not for me.

I need something . . . else. Someone else.

And suddenly, I'm there. I'm at his house. It's a smallish brick thing with a barn mailbox. The yard is neatly mowed and there are yellow and pink tulips out front.

And Alex Belrose is sitting out on the porch in a hoodie that says PURDUE. He leans forward when he sees me.

My phone buzzes in my pocket. I pull it out. I have a new e-mail.
Go around back.

TWELVE
Bad

I know what he's saying.

Don't walk in my front door. Don't be obvious.

But come here.

My hands shake. I shove them into the pockets of my jeans.

I walk three houses down and cut through a lawn toward the alley, which is lined with trees.

And therefore hard to see from the homes on either side.

Good call, Mr. Belrose.

Alex.

Mr. Belrose.

I pause at the gate. It's white and wooden and badly in need of a paint job.

SUCH A GOOD GIRL

Stop.

I hear it in my head like someone is saying it, like someone is actually telling me.

This is it.

This is the line.

Right here.

And if I cross it, I become an entirely different Riley Stone. An entirely different girl. I will not be the good girl, the girl who loves bookstores, the girl who kisses boys because she has to because she's in a play, or the girl who is perfect because that's who she is and what she does.

I will have a secret.

I will have done something wrong.

Really wrong.

For one second, my body feels heavy, and I want to turn around and run. I want to sprint down the alley, as fast as I can, and cut back toward the street where Belrose can't see me and just leave.

But then I press my hands against the wooden gate and it swings open, revealing the backyard, choked with trees and an empty chicken coop and there he is. He is wearing khaki shorts even though it's too cold for them and his hands are jammed into the pocket of his hoodie.

And he's smiling.

Big.

At me.

Just at me.

It's not his teacher smile. It's the Alex smile.

103

"Wanna sit?" he asks, motioning at an Adirondack chair on his back porch.

"Um, yeah." I settle into the chair, sitting my purse down on the wooden planks. He sits too, opposite me, and we look at each other and look away and then look at each other and his eyes are so goddamn green and what am I doing?

"Do you want something to drink?" he asks.

"Sure."

He disappears into his house and comes back a moment later with two sarsaparillas.

"Do you like root beer?" He twists off the top for me, so obviously he doesn't expect me to say no.

It's not my favorite, but I take one anyway. "Sure." It's frosty and cold. I wonder if he has ice cream. We could make root beer floats.

No. That's immature. I'm an adult. I am grown-up. I am almost in college, and Mr. Belrose—Alex—is taking me seriously.

He could have offered me a real beer and I would have said, "Sure," and then I could have made a toast or something, but there isn't a lot you can say about root beer. Which is something you give a kid.

But a real beer—that would have meant something. If he would have given me a real beer, like an equal, I would have taken it, and I would have smiled at him, and that gesture would have said everything, just there, and I would have lifted my beer and said, "To you, Alex," and he would have said, "No, to you," and I would have known he was glad that I was on the same level as he was, and it would have been everything the party with Neta and

SUCH A GOOD GIRL

Kolbie wasn't. He would have been showing me he trusted me, and maybe I would have brought up something about *L'Amant*, and I could have told him how I really did understand the themes of repression and how we need to act on our desires.

We sit in silence for a few seconds.

He takes a sip of his sarsaparilla.

"So."

"Uh, do you want to talk about how great my essay is or something?" My joke feels weak and flat as soon as I say it, and I wish I could take the words back.

He laughs. "That seems like a safe topic."

I feel a smile working its way to my lips, and I don't know if it's because I am happy or because I'm nervous or because my stomach feels like something is alive inside of it. "We don't have to be safe."

His eyes catch mine. "No?"

I shake my head. "No. I'm not exactly the good girl that everyone thinks I am." I take a drink of my root beer, and a little bit dribbles on my chin. I wipe it off quickly, hoping he doesn't notice.

"I've known that for a long time." He looks away from me, into his backyard. "You're more than just a good student. You're better than that."

I cock my head at him. "Better?" What does that mean?

"I think that just sort of reduces you to a few grades and some scholarships. And people are scared of that sort of perfection, aren't they? They have to quantify you somehow to make you safer. So you're a certain sort of girl to them, and then everything is just—easier."

105

"Yeah? And who am I to you?"

He looks at me and presses his lips together. "I don't know yet. But if it's okay with you, I'd kind of like a chance to figure it out."

I feel a little warm. "I think I'd like that too."

I look up at the sky. The sun is starting to go down, and I can hear crickets starting up their insistent nighttime song. It's getting a little chilly, and goose bumps begin to prick up on my arms. "What sort of man are you, then?"

He shifts in his chair. "Would it weird you out if I said I didn't know yet?"

I set my drink down. "Not really. I think sometimes people spend their whole lives just trying to figure out who they are. And I don't know what the big deal is about having to define yourself immediately or even at all. Who says that you should have to discover exactly who you are by the time you graduate from college? I don't think anyone knows by that point."

Belrose leans forward, his elbows on his knees. "You're smart, you know that? And not like everyone has been telling you your whole life, either. But really smart. You see people."

I tuck my hair behind my ears and smile tightly in an attempt to veil how pleased the compliment really makes me. "Thanks."

And I realize that this . . . this is what it's supposed to feel like. Not Jell-O shots in damp Dixie cups. Not some guy who smells like cheap beer and sweat.

This.

I wanted Alex Belrose.

And not in a childish-crush way. Not in the stupid way that

SUCH A GOOD GIRL

everyone kisses in the high school hallways and fights about prom dates and makes out in their parents' basements.

I really wanted him. Truly. So much I can barely stand it. So much it hurts in my chest.

"I'd like to see more of you," Belrose—Alex says. He reaches for me, but then pulls his hand back, like he's unsure how I'll respond. Slowly, I reach out, and I brush my fingers against his. He catches my hand and holds it.

"I'd be okay with that."

"Maybe you could come over and . . . um . . . we could read. Or something. And we could catch up?"

I nod. "Yeah. Of course."

He smiles, and I stand up, and he stands too. He pulls my scarf out of his pocket and loops it around my shoulders, using it to pull me close to him, so our chests are almost touching and I can feel the heat of him near me.

My pulse quickens. I feel his breath on my face.

"I like you, Riley Stone."

"I like you too . . . Alex."

"I like when you call me that." He tugs me a little closer with my scarf. "Can I see you again soon?"

I nod. "Yes."

"Do you promise?" he asks.

"I promise."

He releases the scarf. "Good girl."

107

THIRTEEN
New

"Two suitcases? *Two?*"

Kolbie pants as she lugs the second leather suitcase into my room. "You could have helped."

I cross my arms. "Uh, I asked you to bring over a few outfits, not your entire wardrobe."

Kolbie gives me her sassiest hair flip. "Seriously? Don't exaggerate. You know it would take a moving truck to get all my clothes up here. Plus they wouldn't fit in your pitiful excuse for a closet." She casts her eyes toward my non-walk-in closet, which holds all my clothes quite nicely, thank you very much.

I hold up my palm. "Okay, can you tone down the sass, please? My wardrobe is actually pretty serviceable. I just want to try something new."

SUCH A GOOD GIRL

"Well, your wardrobe isn't pitiful. It just needs expansion. Oh, and I bought you makeup! I'm so excited to be able to make you over!" She does a happy little hop.

"I have makeup." I nod toward my little bathroom, where I have a couple of things I apply to my face every morning. It's very conservative, but it's adequate. I look perfectly presentable.

She unfolds a cosmetic bag across my bed. It looks like an artist's palette. "No, *I* have makeup."

I approach my bed cautiously. What is this girl doing? I asked for new style, not to appear on *What Not to Wear: Kolbie Edition*. I am looking for exploration, not a whole new Riley.

"It's okay," Kolbie says slowly, guiding me to a chair and sitting me down. "It's not a wild animal. It's not going to bite you. Besides, I owe you, don't I?"

"No," I say.

"Please. You were up with me until midnight going over my college applications with me, and I know for a fact you half wrote an entrance essay for Neta last week. The least I can do is fix you up." She tousles my hair, and I resist the urge to smooth it down.

"I'm not, like, fashionably challenged here," I say. "I don't want to go straight to Crazytown. I just want a little flair."

Kolbie begins sharpening an eye pencil. "Girl, I have got you a little flair. Relax, okay? This is going to be fun. And if you hate it, you can go straight back to J.Crew with the rest of your kind, okay?"

"What does that mean?"

"Nothing," she says innocently. "Now, what do you use for an eye primer?"

109

"A what?"

She groans theatrically and makes fists. "I have so much work to do with you. I for real need your foundation, though, because mine is not going to work on that pasty-ass skin of yours. Now stop squirming."

"I'm not even!"

"You are too!"

"Then stop pointing that eye pencil at me like it's a weapon!"

She puts it down and laughs. "Damn, Ri. Has anyone ever told you your room is too clean?" She leans over and unzips her other suitcase, and then pulls out the Bluetooth speaker she brought to study hall and turns it up. "Do your parents care if we have wine?" She pulls out a few little Sutter Home bottles.

I shrug. "If we don't drive, I guess."

The truth is, I don't know what they'd think. But as long as we aren't incredibly obvious I don't think they'd mind. Besides, the last time my mother checked on me in my room, I think I was, like, nine and playing with toy horses and had some sort of accident with red Kool-Aid that resulted in my mother having to replace my carpet.

I unscrew the cap on mine and try a sip. It's a little bitter and sugary all at once. "What is this?"

"Uh, chardonnay, I think." She tries a sip too. "It's good, right?"

"I guess. I don't really know anything about wine. My parents only let me drink a glass on holidays. And at communion at church."

"I thought that was grape juice."

SUCH A GOOD GIRL

I give her a withering look. "Please. The blood of Christ is *not* grape juice at my church."

She holds up a perfectly manicured hand. "Whatever. Hey, I was going to ask you. What's the deal with the sudden makeover request? And you wanting to go to parties and skip class all of a sudden?"

"Because I want to."

Kolbie gives me a look. I know the look. It's basically saying, *Come on, I'm not that stupid.* That is the problem with having smart friends who are not total clichés. In movies, the three popular girls are always, like, traipsing down the hallways at schools in tiny clothes and looking gorgeous and never actually doing schoolwork. But my girls are not just caricatures.

"It's not about a guy," I say. "It doesn't always have to be about a guy."

Lie number one.

"I know it's not."

"I'm just tired of being the same and looking the same. I'm bored. I want to have some fun, you know? Before high school ends? Isn't this supposed to be, like, the best time of our lives and stuff?"

Kolbie takes another sip of her wine and sits it on the end of my dresser. She begins laying the clothes out along my bed. "First of all, no. If high school is the best time of our lives, that's kind of sad. That means you're getting all the good stuff out of the way pretty fast, doesn't it?"

I smile at my friend. She really is brilliant. And of course

111

she doesn't get enough credit for it on account of being super beautiful.

"I guess so. But still. Even that idea . . . doesn't that mean I should be having more fun than I'm having?"

Kolbie starts hanging her clothes along my closet doors. "If you want to have more fun, have more fun. Just do it, you know? Seriously. I'll tell you what. Jamal is going to be in town this weekend, he's bringing one of his good friends. And honestly, it's fun to date. So why don't you come along next time?"

"I told you this wasn't about finding a man."

Kolbie looks back at me over her shoulder. "It doesn't have to be. It's about getting out of the prison you call a comfort zone. So have fun. And if you like the guy, awesome. And if not, well, you hopefully had a good time and you ate some pizza or whatever. And I promise it'll be better than a lame party. Okay?"

I hesitate.

What about Belrose?

What about *Alex*?

But that's why I need to. I can't look like I have any attachment to him whatsoever.

I have to do this. For us.

"I'm in."

Kolbie beams at me. She pushes her hair back into a knot on top of her head, like a ballet dancer.

"Now, the look is professional chic. I am thinking this"— she pulls a pencil skirt off the bed—"with these and these"—she yanks a pair of patterned black tights out of her second suitcase.

SUCH A GOOD GIRL

"And I'm thinking maybe a cute V-neck, fitted, of course, with a scarf."

"I have the scarf. It's special."

I pull the scarf from the night before out of my closet and wrap it around my neck. It still smells like him—just a hint of his cologne lingers.

Kolbie taps a finger on her lips and juts her hip out, considering. "Why that scarf? You wear it all the time."

"This look has to have a little *me* in it, right? Besides, I got it shopping with you and Neta." I bury my fingers in it, daring her to make me take it off.

Kolbie shoves the clothes into my arms. "Okay, okay. Go. Try on. I have three more combos we can go through, and yes, you can borrow these. And I know you don't wear glasses, but it would be totally on point if we could get you some nonprescription frames. I'm thinking a round black plastic frame? Yes?"

I make a face. "I am not going to be *one of those girls*."

"There is nothing wrong with being one of those girls, Riley. Stop being judgy. Listen to the master." She points at herself. "Wear things because they make you feel good about yourself. Not because you think you should or shouldn't."

"Are you going to write a self-help book in the near future?" I ask innocently. "I think Oprah has it covered, but if you want to go for that, I mean, shoot for the stars—"

"Are you going to keep being a bitch to the girl who is going to do your mascara in about ten minutes?"

I laugh. I can't help it. I love Kolbie. "Point taken."

113

"Good. Now try on those clothes before we worry about the makeup, I guess. And then we're going to Instagram the hell out of this."

I smile a little to myself. Normally I wouldn't let her put anything on my Instagram. I reserve it for cute coffee mugs and perfectly round waffles and generally keep my face out of it.

But maybe, just maybe, someone important will be checking in.

FOURTEEN
Dinner

I cut through the alley again.

It's safer that way. I come from the opposite direction, and I wear a big black hat with my hair tucked up under it and a large coat.

I don't see anyone in the alley.

The door is unlocked, so I let myself in through the back door, into a den sort of room with a squishy brown leather couch and a fireplace. The décor is spare and a bit lowbrow, and not at all what I'd expect from Jacqueline Belrose—it's actually a little kitschy, all HOME SWEET HOME signs and flowers, like maybe it was lifted out of an outdated *Good Housekeeping*. A squatty little table holds a cookbook and a bouquet of dusty plastic flowers.

"Hey!"

AMANDA K. MORGAN

I hear Alex's voice through a door. "Hey," I call. "It's me."

"Come into the kitchen!" he calls back, and I follow a red runner rug through the den and into a little kitchen with a small white table and yellow curtains. Two matching rooster salt and pepper shakers sit in the middle of the table, wings extended and necks out.

"Riley!" He sees me and grins, wrapping me in a quick hug, his arms around my body, and then releases me. "Sit. Please. I'm almost done." He pulls out a chair for me at the kitchen table, which is . . . set for two.

He pours me a small glass of red wine, then swirls it around, lifting it to his nose. "Do you like Malbec?"

I bite back a smile. I have no idea what Malbec is. "I love Malbec."

"I wasn't expecting you for a while," he says. "I thought you had cheerleading practice."

"I pretended I was sick and asked my cocaptain to take over," I tell him, and almost immediately regret it. Why was I so eager? Why did I do that? He's used to girls falling all over him. I should be different. I am special, after all. But instead of practice, I'd gone home to fix up my makeup exactly the way Kolbie taught me (well, a toned-down version of the way Kolbie taught me) and get pretty for Alex Belrose.

"That's sweet," he says. "You didn't have to do that."

"I just wasn't feeling it anyway."

He pours another glass of wine and takes a sip. "I'm glad you're here, Riley. I wanted to see you."

I want to smile and duck my head, but I force myself to meet his eyes. "Me too, Alex."

116

SUCH A GOOD GIRL

"God, I love when you say my name."

His voice sends shivers down my spine. "Yeah?" I grab my glass of wine and take a sip. "That's okay?"

"It's good." He turns to open the oven, and a warm, citrusy smell fills the room. "I think it's done."

"What did you make?" I ask. I can't believe he cooked for me. He must—he must actually *like* me. *Like* like me. I have the jitters. I busy myself with spreading the yellow napkin next to my plate across my lap. This is like a date. A real date. This is what couples do.

"Lemon-pepper salmon," he says, pulling an oven mitt over his hand. He pulls the tray out. "I hope you like fish."

"I do," I say, saying a silent thank-you that he didn't cook tilapia, which I personally think is too gross to eat. "Thank you so much for cooking."

"You're welcome." He takes my plate and hands it back with a salmon fillet and a few spears of asparagus. "My grandfather was actually a chef, so most of my family can cook really well."

"That's cool. Did he have his own restaurant?"

Alex sits down across from me with his own plate. "Yeah. It was called the Belrose. Creative, right? Anyway, it did really well until he died. My dad tried to take it over, but it wasn't the same without my grandfather. We were struggling to keep it afloat, so my dad sold it."

"I'm sorry."

"Yeah. Me too." He smiles, but it's missing some of the happiness that should be attached to it. "My grandmother, I guess, was

117

the saddest. She is the only one of us who can't cook. Like, at all. She did all the financials for the restaurant because she would burn, like, *everything*. She tries to microwave something and it starts on fire."

I start to laugh. "That sounds like my mom, honestly." I take a forkful of salmon. It's delicious and flavorful, and it really does taste like something I would order at a fancy restaurant. "One time she tried to make my brother chocolate chip cookies and she started a fire in the oven. She forgot to add the flour."

Alex points at me with his fork, a piece of asparagus speared onto the end. "My grandfather actually kept an extra fire extinguisher in the kitchen specifically because of my grandmother. I mean, he forbid her from ever going in there, but every once in a while she'd try to make coffee or something and bring about world-ending fumes. Like, you could die if you went near. It was a hazard."

I giggle. "With coffee?"

He nods solemnly. "You have no idea. She's in a rest home now, and the nurses won't even let her try *tea*. To be fair, they probably don't let anyone, but they actually have good reason with her."

"Do you see her often?"

He pauses while he finishes chewing. "Not like I'd like. She's in Oregon."

"That's hard."

"Yeah."

We're quiet for a minute. I'm lucky. Even though my family feels remarkably distant sometimes, they're all close and here and

SUCH A GOOD GIRL

alive. Most people experience death in some major way by the time they're in high school, it seems. But I haven't. I've been charmed.

Perfect Riley Stone and Her Perfect Life.

"This is really good," I tell him. "Like, really, really good."

"Thanks," he says. "It's one of my signature dishes."

"I'm glad you can cook," I say. "Because it's not one of my strengths."

Alex pretends to be shocked. He lets his fork drop from his fingers. It clatters onto his plate. "I thought you didn't have any *not-strengths.*"

"I have several not-strengths," I confess, solemn.

"Tell me," he says. "Because right now, I sort of think you're perfect." He reaches across the table and brushes my hand with the very tips of his fingers, and it starts this strange sort of reaction in my body, beginning in my hand and then running through my veins and settling somewhere in my lower belly.

I bite my lip. "I sort of think you're perfect too."

"So give me a confession," he urges, his fingers still on the back of my hand. "Tell me something."

I want him to run his hand up my arm. I want more of those fingers. I want to tell him that.

"Well, I'm very bad at riding bicycles."

He smiles at me, anticipating a joke. "How can you be bad at riding a bicycle? Isn't that a rite of passage for kids everywhere?"

"I just suck. I think I have a bad center of balance or something. I just can't do it. It's stupid."

"You're lucky, you know." He stops stroking my hand, and I

119

long for his fingers back. I want to grasp at them, but I will my hands to stay still on the table.

"Lucky? How?" I look at his green eyes, the scruff growing on his cheeks.

His lips.

"I'm an excellent bicyclist. I could teach you."

"Teach me?" I ask. I smile even harder, smile from deep in my chest. I imagine his hands around my waist, steadying me. "When?"

"Maybe we meet in the middle of the night," he says. His hand slips under mine from across the table and squeezes. "Maybe we put the bikes in the back of my truck and go out to the country. And I can teach you there. And we'll get dusty out on the dirt roads and ride until the sun comes up."

I squeeze back. "That sounds perfect," I breathe.

"And you'll cook for me," Alex says.

I move back slightly. "Wait, what?" That was . . . a leap.

"Please?" he pleads. He blinks. His eyelashes are gorgeous. He's gorgeous. "Next time. Tell me what ingredients you need and cook for me. I promise to eat it even if it's terrible."

"The only thing I know how to make is, like, the little mini pizzas that Ms. Archer taught us to put together in Family and Consumer Sciences last year," I say. Which, of course, I got an A on. That and monkey bread, but I can't make Alex monkey bread and call it a meal. And I can make a mean plate of brownies, but that leaves me in the same place as monkey bread.

That's not to say I haven't had a yoga-pants-and-monkey-bread day or eight.

120

SUCH A GOOD GIRL

Alex releases my hands and stands from the table. He rummages through a kitchen door and comes back with a pad and paper. "Okay, Riley. Tell me what you need for mini pizzas. I'll bring back the ingredients, and you cook them for me. Okay?"

"Um, okay." I smile. "Will you help?"

He pretends to think. "A little. Maybe. If you're good."

I laugh. "I'm always good."

He watches me. "Are you, though?"

I duck my head, unsure of the answer. I am, but I'm not. I'm not. I am.

My heart does this strange twisty thing.

"Ingredients?" he presses, and I list them off the best I can remember, and promise to meet him again in two days.

This time, when I say good-bye, he touches me. His hands touch my back, and trace up and down. I stare at his lips and I tilt my chin upward, but he doesn't kiss me. My hands touch his shoulders tentatively and slide down to his chest. He is thin but all hard muscle.

"Soon," he promises.

I leave, full and starving at the same time.

Things to Know About Riley Stone:

- In third grade, Riley Stone was caught cheating on a spelling test. Because it was her first offense, she received a zero on the test but was not suspended or given detention.
- Riley's teacher suggested that Riley was under too much stress and called her parents in for a special conference. She was worried about Riley's personal development and wanted her parents to understand the amount of pressure their daughter was putting on herself to succeed.
- Riley never cheated again.
- Sometimes, even girls who do everything right make mistakes.

FIFTEEN
Italian

"I am going to make my pizza in the shape of a dinosaur," Alex announces. "And it will definitely kick your pizza's ass."

"Mine is definitely going to be cooler than that," I say, trying to roll out the dough properly. Honestly, I'm not even sure I've made the dough right, or if a pizza in the shape of a dinosaur would cook evenly. But I don't care. I'm happy in a strange, jittery way that I've never been happy before, and these pizzas will be perfect even if they cook black.

"How can you beat a dinosaur?" he asks, pretending to be offended. "You can't."

I grin at him. I grin at him all the time. It's hard in class, because all I want to do is grin at him, but I have to be studious and

AMANDA K. MORGAN

quiet and uninterested and sit in the same seat and do the work like I'm not going to his house at night. So I bite at the inside of my cheeks and grip my pencil a bit harder and think about later, when I'll be all his and he'll be all mine.

"I can," I say. "Easy."

"How?" he demands.

"A baby sea otter, maybe." I pull the dough into two pieces and toss him half.

"So," he says. "You're going to beat my dinosaur with sheer adorableness?"

I began shaping the dough with my hands. "It's a pretty fool-proof plan. You have to admit."

"It's so good I want to help." Alex abandons his lump of dough in the flour and stands next to me. Very, very close. I smile up at him. He's a floury mess, and I know I am too. His normally perfect hair has a dusting of the fine white powder in it, and there is just a smudge above his left eyebrow.

I'm not a very neat cook.

"How do you intend to improve on this?" I ask, gesturing at the vaguely otterlike shape that could also be a very good eggplant.

He steps behind me and puts his hands over mine. "Like this. Let the master work. I had a solid B in pottery, Riley."

I giggle. "Show me," I say.

"Well, you have to work with me." His breath is hot on my neck. His fingers interlace with mine, and we're both working the dough together. "How is this like an otter?"

126

SUCH A GOOD GIRL

"Like this," he says, and squishes it into an unrecognizable lump.

"Alex!" I cry, and spin around. I push at him with my doughy hands. "You ruined my otter-pizza!"

He doesn't laugh.

He doesn't move, either.

He's just there, close, looking down at me. He's not smiling. He's inches away, and he steps closer, so our bodies are touching.

We're touching.

I reach back, my hands trying to find purchase on his counter. "Um, Alex?"

He touches my chin, very gently. "Riley," he breathes.

And then he's all the way against me and his mouth is against mine and he's kissing me. He's kissing me nice and soft and slow, and I'm kissing him back the same way, my eyes closed, but my heart is doing something crazy, hammering like I'm going to die, right here, while Alex is kissing me.

He pulls away. "Are you okay?" he whispers, his lips next to my ear. His hand slides to the back of my neck.

"Yes," I whisper back. "I'm okay."

I am.

He kisses my neck. He kisses the bit of my chest that is exposed above my shirt.

And then Alex Belrose lifts me up onto the counter. He steps between my legs.

"You," he says, "are gorgeous, Riley."

And then he kisses me more. Pretty soon, I forget to think

about what I'm doing and his tongue slips into my mouth and he isn't so gentle anymore but I don't care because my hands aren't hanging onto the counter anymore either. They're on him.

And that is the story of my first real kiss.

Also, we ordered pizza.

SIXTEEN
Waiting

"You'll have to wait for me tonight," I tell Alex, my voice just above a whisper.

I've caught him in between classes, and I'm bending over his desk, frowning at a scholarship application. I point at a blank space, like I'm asking him a question.

He looks at me, his brows drawing together. "Wait?"

He's not used to waiting. He's used to getting what he wants.

"I can't skip cheerleading again," I murmur, moving my fingers to the next field, like this is just a normal discussion and we're just people, normal people. "I've already missed three practices. The girls are getting suspicious. So just hang on, and I'll be over after. Okay?"

He hesitates, and I know he wants to tell me no, that I should skip cheerleading practice and spend the time with him. But we're both sensible people. Sensible people who will do sensible things and not get caught.

Sensible people who know this is wrong by everyone else's standards.

But not by ours.

"I'll miss you," he murmurs. He casts a glance toward the doorway, but no students filter in. "What will I do without you?"

"I'll be fast. I'm head cheerleader, remember? I run the practice. Let me make sure we're good on our routines, and I'll be over before you know it."

Alex points to something on the application, and I fill in the bubbles above his finger without thinking, the marks messy and outside the lines. "Have your . . . has your family mentioned how late you're getting home?"

I choke back a short laugh. "They have not noticed. They don't ask where I am. I'm the good kid, remember? Ethan was the troubled one."

Alex smiles wryly. "You're *very* good." But the tone of his voice is slick and suggests something different and I suddenly feel warm and strange and I wish we were at his house and he was kissing me again.

That's all we've done. Kiss.

I think I'm getting good at it.

Alex clears his throat. "Just finish the second and third pages at home, and then drop it by tomorrow, okay, Riley?"

SUCH A GOOD GIRL

I glance up. Emilio Rivera has dumped his bag onto the floor and is digging around in it, throwing crumpled papers out on the tiles. Probably the extra-credit work that Alex assigned last class. Three points for writing a two-paragraph report on I-can't-remember-what. A-students weren't eligible, so I didn't bother to write it down.

I nod and gather up the pages, very neatly, taking my time. I wouldn't have hurried before "us."

I won't hurry now.

I tuck the scholarship pages into a folder, slide the folder into my bag, and don't check to see if Alex is watching me as I leave his classroom. I know it doesn't matter if he is.

Because he's mine.

All mine.

I head in the direction of the gymnasium, stick my backpack into my locker, and slip into my cheerleading gear. I'm the first one there, as usual, but before long Neta shows up, and then Bella Cooper, the cocaptain, who takes over when I'm sick. Mrs. Hernandez, the cheerleading coach, only shows up when she can, but she trusts me to run most practices. I've been in gymnastics and cheer since I was a really little girl, and I'm very good at it. And despite the fact that I have been avoiding it, I do love it. A lot.

"Riley!" Bella says, bouncing up to me as I stretch out. "Are you feeling better?"

I smile up at her from a frog position, taking her in. Bella is solid and perfect in about every way, and I try to stand her the best I can. "Yeah. Thanks for asking. Get stretched out okay? I want a good, hard practice today."

131

She puts her hands on her hips and looks down at me. "Are you sure? Maybe you should ease into it. You've been delicate and all." Her tone is peppy, but I've been cheering with her since fourth grade, so I can hear the slight accusatory tone.

"I'm sure she can handle it." Neta plops down next to me into a butterfly stretch, pulling her feet in.

I smile up at Bella. "I've got it," I confirm.

Bella is the type of person who would run a cheerleading practice like we were in a daycare. I'm all for kindness and everything, but if it were her, we'd spend half the practice sitting in a circle on the gym floor holding hands and humming "Kumbaya" at a friendly volume. She thinks I push the team too hard, but that's also why we're good. If I left her in charge for too long, she'd petition to have us removed from competitions on the basis that she wants to be friends with everyone and doesn't like hurting anyone's feelings.

Of course, Bella used to be a lot more like me, but ever since her little brother was put into a juvenile delinquent facility three years ago she's insistent on being very amiable all the time. I personally think she developed the character trait as a coping strategy.

When the whole team is on the floor, I raise my voice a little. Everyone turns toward me. I know how to command power without yelling.

I feel a smile in the muscles of my lips, but I tamp it down.

"All right, girls. Get a stretching partner and count off, okay? As soon as you're done, we're in for some tumbling practice. I know it's basic, but we don't have room for sloppy stuff right now. Then,

SUCH A GOOD GIRL

we'll do some jumps, and we'll take a short break and do some stunting. Okay? I want everything super clean today. We don't have any room for injuries. Everything *will* be tight for the games, and we're going to petition to get more competitions. We'll finish with some cheers and chants as usual, and I need to go over some final thoughts."

The group finishes their stretches and lines up on the black line running the length of the gymnasium, and we begin counting off cartwheels and handsprings. We always do this—start simple. Keep it clean. And then it gets more complex. I pull off a neat back handspring followed by a roundoff back handspring, and Neta whoops and gives me a high five.

"Looks good, Stone!" she says.

"Thanks!" I smile. "Give it a shot!"

She nods and bounces a couple of times and executes the roundoff-back-handspring combo perfectly.

"Gorgeous," I tell her, and she flips her ponytail.

There is no room for Alex in my head during cheerleading. One false move, and someone could be seriously hurt. He sneaks into my mind a couple of times, but I kick him right back out.

There is plenty of room for Alex *after* cheerleading, naturally. There is plenty of room for me in his house. In his arms.

"You're looking great," Neta tells me halfway through practice, when I give the team its second water break. She pats me on the butt.

I smile back at her. I feel good. "You too, Neta."

In fact, I barely even think of Alex.

133

At least, I don't until Fatima Patel pokes me in the arm after a single-twist basket toss. "Hey," she whispers. "Don't look now—but I think Mr. Belrose is checking us out." She giggles and throws her thick black braid over her shoulder.

I look toward the double doors that lead into the hallway of the high school, and there he is: Alex Belrose, in a T-shirt and shorts, like maybe he's been working out in the weight room or something, his arms crossed over his chest, a smile on his face.

And I can't tell if he's smiling because of me . . . or he's smiling because of everyone.

"Finish your jumps, girls!" I bark. "Toe-touches! Five, six, seven, eight!"

There is suddenly more giggling than necessary for something so simple. And then, of course, the team executes the jumps flawlessly.

"Okay. Herkies, then."

I join the girls, and we jump together. I don't look toward the doorway, but I can feel Belrose there, watching.

"Did he see?" Fatima asks, flicking a sweaty piece of hair that has escaped from her braid off her neck. Her pretty cheerleader smile is perched in place and she looks gorgeous, as usual.

That is Fatima, of course. She isn't a great student—she scores Cs, usually—is perpetually late to class, and always has a button in the wrong place or a shoelace untied—but she looks incredible doing it, and actually, quite secretly, puts in a lot of work on her I-woke-up-like-this selfies that she runs through at least three filters.

I feel hot, thick jealousy in my chest that makes it almost impos-

SUCH A GOOD GIRL

sible to breathe. "Again!" I shout, and they're jumping again, and I know Alex hasn't left the doorway, and everyone is jumping extra hard, trying to look good for him, and they're *my* cheerleaders, so of course they do.

I want them to stop.

"Okay, everyone. Let's break for water." I clap, and they head to the bleachers—and then to the door.

Where Alex is standing, his arm outstretched, hand out, the *not*-Belrose grin on his face that's supposed to be for me.

Just for me.

And my entire team runs past on the way to the water fountain and high-fives him. Including Neta.

When they all have perfectly good water bottles in the bleachers.

Better water bottles, actually, because everyone knows that water fountains are disgusting places where germs go to live and breed and create mutant diseases than can take out entire populations.

Pathetic.

I walk to the bleachers by myself and grab my purple water bottle. Neta comes back to sit by me.

"Wow, Ri, you couldn't even line up for a high five?" Neta asks. She settles down beside me on the bleachers. "I mean, you have to admit he's hot."

"Whatever. Can we just get back to practicing?" I push away from the bleachers. "Stunting, please."

"That was barely a break," Claire Meadows mutters.

"Line up, please." I clap. "Now, let's go. No more distractions."

I don't glance back at the door, but I don't make practice

135

short, either. I make it long. Extra long. We go through stunts and cheers and do a second round of jumps. The team drags before the end of it. My legs scream with every additional movement, but I don't care.

When I finally let the team go and I'm taking off my shoes, my phone vibrates. It's an e-mail.

Are you coming over?

The jealousy curls around my heart and squeezes.

This is all too far. This whole relationship. Him and me. Everything is wrong. Everything. And I can't handle this. I can't handle him and me and the cheerleaders and the high fives and all this bullshit.

It's just *wrong* and it's been wrong the whole time and I've been an absolute *fool.*

No thank you, I e-mail back.

And then I turn off my phone.

I am done.

SEVENTEEN
To Play

French class is French class.

Alex is Mr. Belrose.

I am a student. A straight-A student and head cheerleader. Someone who made a mistake and knows it.

I am a student who does not put up with anyone flirting with other girls. Especially not right in front of her.

Mr. Belrose hands out our essays. I haven't let myself e-mail him or see him. I am good. I am the good girl everyone always thought I was.

He pauses a millisecond longer at my desk. A millisecond only I notice. I face straight forward. Thea giggles and tries to draw his attention.

He doesn't even look at her.

"Verb forms," Mr. Belrose says. "Let's start with, uh, Miss Stone. Riley—'to love.'"

"Oh. Hmm. I think it's *jouer*."

I fix him with an icy stare.

I have given him the French word for "play." Because that's what he's done to me.

Play. I am his little game.

"*Aimer*, Mademoiselle Stone. Incorrect. Surprising."

I stare at him, arms crossed over my chest, daring him to question me further.

He doesn't. He moves on to Keatra, and then to Cay, then Garrett, and Teri Von Millhouse.

He doesn't come back to me.

I don't meet his eyes.

And when the bell rings, I pack up my books.

"Riley, I'll need you to stay after class, please," Mr. Belrose says. He's not asking, either. His voice is a quiet command, and I want nothing more than to walk out the door with the rest of the students.

"Why?" I ask. My tone isn't the respectful one I save for teachers, either. But he isn't just my teacher anymore.

He doesn't answer, only watches as the students file out of the room. I watch them too, my backpack slung over one arm. I drop it on the floor as Mr. Belrose follows Thea to the door and closes it after her.

And then we're alone.

In his classroom.

SUCH A GOOD GIRL

During school hours.

Alarms go off in my head.

"You're ignoring my e-mails," he says.

I tilt my head at him. I had thought Alex Belrose was a smart guy. But he's not acting like one. Not at all. "Well, I haven't wanted to respond, particularly. Or see you."

"Can I ask why?" His voice is quiet. And a little dangerous.

"How many special students do you have?"

"Excuse me?" He leans in, his hand next to his ear.

"How many goddamn girls are you inviting over?" I ask. "One for every high five?"

He smiles, his mouth pulled up just a little farther on one side than the other. "Is that what all this is about?" He motions at me.

I stand up a little straighter. "What do you think it's about?"

"You think—you think there are others, Riley?"

"How am I supposed to know, Alex?" I snap, and then hate myself for using his name. Damn it. He's not Alex anymore. He's Mr. Belrose. My teacher.

Not someone who is fun to kiss.

He takes a step toward me, and I fight not to step back. I have to be strong.

"You're the only one, Riley," he whispers. "There's no one else. I swear to God. There's no one else in the world."

"How am I supposed to believe that?" I look at his eyes, but he doesn't blink. He looks at me straight-on.

"Because you're the only one I'd ever take this kind of risk for,

139

AMANDA K. MORGAN

Riley. And I can't stop thinking about you. Not for one second. And it's driving me insane to know you're angry at me."

He reaches out and links his fingers in mine. I don't pull away. His hands are shaking.

"Will you come back to me? Please?" he pleads.

I feel my insides softening.

"I only came to your practice to see you. I'm sorry for upsetting you. Besides, I have something really special planned. Just promise you'll come see it tonight. If you hate it, you can leave." His fingers tighten on my hand.

I hesitate, dropping my head.

"Please, Riley." His fingers find the bottom of my chin and lift it, and he's staring into me. "I'm begging you. Please do this. For me."

I nod, even though my stomach feels cold and hard, like I've just had a gallon of too-cold water. "I guess. But this is for me. Not for you."

He smiles at me. "God, I want to kiss you so badly right now."

"Do it." I dare him. My words are hard and angry and I want him to but I don't. I want him to hold me and never let go and I want him to leave me alone forever.

I'm not entirely sure if I forgive him.

The classroom door swings open behind us, and he drops my hand and my chin like he was never holding me and jams them both in his pockets, like his skin has some residue left on it, some evidence that he was touching me.

"Due Monday," he reminds me, like that's what we were discussing all along. "And remember the bibliography."

140

SUCH A GOOD GIRL

I scoff.

What a terrible cover.

Like Riley Stone would *ever* forget a bibliography.

I walk out.

No looking back.

Riley Stone never looks back.

EIGHTEEN
Gifts

It is dark tonight, and unseasonably cold. I vary the times when I arrive at the Belrose house, but I don't think any neighbors have seen me. I dress quietly, and I wear hats pulled low over my face, but even so I change where I park, and my clothing, too. Tonight, I arrived well after the sun went down, and the cloudy night sky hid me well. Summer is barely gone, but the air already feels like winter. It's strange. Everyone says it's due to climate change, because normally at this time everyone would still be wearing shorts and running their sprinklers and lolling about on their lawns with glasses of lemonade on Sundays.

It's lucky for me that the early cold is keeping everyone indoors.

And there was no one to see me slip toward the dark home.

SUCH A GOOD GIRL

There are no lights on in the Belrose house.

But when I push on the back door, it swings in, like he was waiting for me. And that is where I am right now.

I stand in the den, alone. I unwrap my scarf from my neck. Something is different.

"Hello?" I call, and I take a step inside. The house isn't completely dark . . . there's a faint glow coming from the hallway. I close the door softly behind me, my senses blinking on high alert.

My heart beats a little oddly. Is everything okay? I tiptoe toward the faint light. Why is everything off? Alex asked me to come. Did he forget? Is he gone?

Is Jacqueline somehow back and he wants me to leave?

I move toward the glow, my heart beating thunderously in my ears.

Oh.

Oh.

Several gorgeous, white, long-stemmed candles line the hallway. I follow the path down the hallway and through the little kitchen where we've cooked together, and finally, into his living room. And there he is. Alex. He looks at me, over his arm, which is on the back of the couch.

"Come sit with me, Riley."

No one has ever lit candles for me before. I thought it was something that only happened in movies. Silly movies. But he did it.

I walk to the front of the couch and curl into the crook of his arm, so that my back is against his chest.

143

AMANDA K. MORGAN

"Hello," I purr against him.

"Hello," he says, smoothing my hair back. "I'm happy you're here."

"I am too."

And I am. The strange feeling in my stomach is all but gone. He wraps his arms around me and pulls me tight. "I have something for you," he whispers.

"You don't have to get me things," I murmur. And I mean it. I'm not the type of girl who needs *things*. But all the same, I'm excited.

"Close your eyes and hold out your hands," he whispers in my ear. He untangles his arms, and he places something in my palms . . . something light. "Okay. You can open them."

My eyes open. In my hands is a small rectangular box wrapped in light periwinkle paper, tied with a pretty white bow.

"A present! What is it?" I turn it over and look at the bottom, as if that will give me some sort of clue that I'm missing.

"You'll have to open it," he says. He touches my arm. "I hope you like it."

I slide my index finger under the paper, opening it neatly. He's given me something. Something special. He's lit candles and he's given me a real gift, something I can hold on to and keep. I unfold the paper, and there's a dark blue velvet box inside. Is it jewelry? I give him a quizzical look.

He smiles and nods.

I lift the top off the box.

It's a necklace.

144

SUCH A GOOD GIRL

He's given me a necklace. It is a tiny wooden chess piece on a delicate chain. A king.

My fingers stray to the hollow below my throat, where the little charm will hang when I wear it.

"It's gorgeous," I tell him.

He works the clasp apart. "Hold up your hair," he tells me, and I gather it all up while he drapes the necklace around my neck. The wood is cool against my skin. "I got this at a little shop in Paris," he says, "just along the Seine."

I let my hair drop and turn to face him, my fingers running up and down the little chain. "It's from Paris?" I breathe. I've never owned anything from Paris. Not anything from out of the country, until you count the little sand candle my aunt brought me from Puerto Vallarta.

"The man who owns the shop makes the charms by hand, and his vision is slowly failing, but his jewelry, it's all beautiful. It all has these tiny imperfections, you see, so they're all completely one of a kind. And I used to love chess when I was little. I played it against my grandfather at night after he closed the restaurant." He touches the necklace with a knuckle, and then leans in, his lips just barely grazing mine. "Do you like it, Riley?" he asks, his lips moving against mine.

"I adore it."

I'm not lying. I love it all. I love the candles and the necklace and his lips and his arms and being his. I smile, and I smile with my whole entire heart, in a way that I don't think I have ever smiled before.

145

I don't let myself think about how he originally bought the necklace for anyone else.

"Will you think of me whenever you wear it?"

I nod.

"I'm so sorry I made you feel insecure," he whispers.

Wait. Insecure? No one has ever—*ever*—called Riley Stone insecure.

I am *not* insecure.

I just have standards that do not involve whoever I am seeing high-fiving entire teams of girls who are doing cheers for him, that's all.

But then Alex's hands are on my back and his lips are on mine and I forget that maybe, just maybe, I'm a little insulted and I remember he has given me a necklace and we are us again and everything is going to be okay.

I know it is.

NINETEEN
Rules

Rules for dating your teacher:

- Don't skip multiple cheerleading practices. This goes double when you are the head cheerleader.
- Don't look at him any more than normal. Or less than normal. Don't smile at him.
- Ace your homework.
- Don't stab any of the girls who swoon over your teacher in the eye holes, no matter how tempting. This goes double for Thea Arnold.

He slipped a note in between the pages of my homework.

Life is better with you.

AMANDA K. MORGAN

Tonight. I left my response beneath his grading binder when no one else was around.

We leave each other these little notes. We don't sign them. We don't write like ourselves. But we know who they're from. No one else would send me notes the way he does.

I sneak to his house at night. On nights when I don't have practice, I slip into my track tights and sneakers and walk over there, taking my time. My parents don't even care that I'm gone. I'm a busy girl, after all. I always have this fund-raiser or that volunteer event or this mock trial event or that.

Or *this* forbidden love affair or *that* forbidden love affair.

Or just the one.

Tonight, Alex is reading me French poetry. He isn't just paging through a book, though—he's copied his favorites into a worn-out leather-bound notebook, and the pages are a little yellowed and the penciled entries are smudged, like he's read through them a hundred times.

"You're like someone out of a story," I tell him, paging through the handwritten poetry. "You actually copied all these down?"

He nods. "It's what I did to practice my French, actually. And I thought that they were nice."

"They are nice," I tell him, and he smiles at me.

I prop my head on my hand, elbow resting on the floor. "Read me another. A love poem."

"A love poem? Are you trying to tell me something, Riley Stone?" He smiles at me over his notebook.

148

SUCH A GOOD GIRL

I roll over and look at him upside down. "Are you going to read me another pretty poem or not, Alex?"

He leans over and kisses me on the chin, then pages through his book.

"Aha! Here it is."

I turn right side up. He's pointing at a page with a corner folded down.

"It's called '*Les Roses de Saadi*,'" he tells me. "It's by this famous French poet—Marceline Desbordes-Valmore."

> *J'ai voulu ce matin te rapporter des roses;*
> *Mais j'en avais tant pris dans mes ceintures closes*
> *Que les noeuds trop serrés n'ont pu les contenir.*
>
> *Les noeuds ont éclaté. Les roses envolées*
> *Dans le vent, à la mer s'en sont toutes allées.*
> *Elles ont suivi l'eau pour ne plus revenir;*
>
> *La vague en a paru rouge et comme enflammée.*
> *Ce soir, ma robe encore en est tout embaumée . . .*
> *Respires-en sur moi l'odorant souvenir.*

"Tell me what it's about?" I ask. "Roses and the wind?"

"It's love being roses. And the wind tossing them about. This girl brings roses to her love, but the sash she has tied them with splits and they blow to the sea, and they turn the waves red."

AMANDA K. MORGAN

"That's kind of sad."

"It is," he tells me.

"Why did you read me a sad love poem?"

He rolls on top of me and spreads little kisses along my neck. "So I can make you happy again."

Alex kisses me on the mouth, hard, so I can feel his teeth, and I wrap my arms and legs around him. I want him, and I want all of him, and I want my clothes off and to be in his bed, but I know that's not now. Not yet.

We've talked about it. A few weeks ago I hadn't had a real kiss, and now I'm talking about sex. Real sex, and not the giggly way I talk about it with Neta and Kolbie, but with someone who cooks for me and gives me jewelry and reads me French poetry.

"Are you ready?" he asks me, looking into my eyes, and I know what he's asking because his hand is on the button of my jeans.

I kiss him, hard, but then I turn and shake my head no into his shoulder. "Soon," I promise, but I'm lying because this is big and I'm not ready. I want to be ready. But that's a lot and that's moving fast and there's just a lot in this relationship that I haven't really thought through.

I feel him smile against my mouth. "I'm going to wait for you, Riley Stone," he says. "I promise. Do you know why?" His hip bones dig into mine, and I want him.

I do.

"Why?" I ask.

"Because I am absolutely falling in love with you."

150

SUCH A GOOD GIRL

I pull away and look into his eyes, but he's just looking down at me. I feel the weight of the necklace on my throat. "Do you mean that?"

He nods and kisses me again. "More than anything, Riley." He rolls off of me, and for a moment we're just next to each other on the living room floor. "Pretty soon, you're going to be eighteen. And you'll have graduated. And do you know what that means?"

"What?" I ask.

He smiles and touches my hair. "We can be together everywhere. Not just in secret. You won't have to sneak through the alley anymore. I can take you to the movies and to restaurants and visit you at school and you can sleep over and no one can say anything, ever."

"And Jacqueline?" I ask.

And then I hold my breath.

It's the first time I've ever mentioned Jacqueline.

Ever.

"I don't think Jacqueline's ever coming back. And if she does, we're as good as over." His voice is flat.

I want to ask him more, but the lack of emotion in his voice is strange. It excites me.

He's mine.

Really mine.

I don't think anyone in the history of the entire world has ever had a love like we have.

151

This is all going to work.

"Never leave me, okay, Riley?" Alex says. His tone is soft, and he tugs on a piece of my hair.

"I won't," I whisper. "It's us, forever." I put my hand on his heart, and he lifts my palm to his lips.

Things to Know About Riley Stone:

- Riley's parents were chairs of several local charities. Family outings often consisted of Saturday evening volunteer events, where Riley made several contacts.
- Riley's favorite charity is the Humane Society. However, Mr. and Mrs. Stone do not like the smell of the Humane Society kennels, so their daughter rarely had the opportunity to volunteer.
- Riley was never allowed to own a pet.
- Riley won several of her scholarships through very charitable organizations. Her entire college experience was paid off by the time she was a junior in high school, but she continued to apply for scholarships "for the experience."
- And, of course, the prestige.
- In spite of Riley's direction and planning, she has not yet chosen a major or path in life. Options include the following:
  + Doctor
  + Diplomat
  + Business owner
  + Event planner
  + President
  + Fashion designer
  + YouTuber
  + Cheerleading coach/entrepreneur

TWENTY
Fine

You're everything. Don't forget.

The note has been slipped into my locker.

I leave my finished scholarship application on his desk. "Section twelve B," I say. "I had a question."

He opens the booklet.

Tonight?

I have written the note on a bright green Post-it.

"Actually, I think we're all caught up, so nothing tonight."

I step back from his desk, stunned. Caught up? What about the note? What about us?

He looks up, but his eyes travel past me, to the door. He shuts the scholarship booklet. "This looks good, Riley. Can you turn it in before next week? That's the deadline."

"Yes, Mr. Belrose."

I turn around, and Mrs. Sanchez, the carpentry teacher, is standing in the doorway. "Alex! Will you and Jacqueline be coming to the faculty mixer next week? I heard she's back in town! I just adore her. She's so charming."

Slow flames start in my stomach and climb to my heart, and for a moment, I hate Mrs. Sanchez a little, even though I've always admired her before, based on the fact that she's dominating a male-dominated field. She's this total grandmotherly type and looks like she could turn around and pull cookies out of the oven at any moment, but instead she teaches carpentry and shows high school students how to build things. Of course, I also heard she has an insane temper and almost got fired five years ago when she threw a hammer against the wall when someone questioned her knowledge of table saws, but maybe you get that way from years of systemic sexism.

"I'm not sure. I'll ask," Mr. Belrose says, but his voice sounds normal, not like he's being torn apart inside like I currently am.

I force myself to calmly put my scholarship application in my backpack and walk to my locker, then into the bathroom near the stairwell on the first floor.

Slow.

Steady.

Calm.

SUCH A GOOD GIRL

I look in the mirror.

Jacqueline?

Back?

Not a big deal.

He's going to get rid of her.

The only reason he was cold to me was because he didn't want Mrs. Sanchez to see.

It's all very clear, of course.

Calm.

I smile at myself in the mirror, but it looks wrong—like I'm peeling back my lips to get a peek at my teeth.

I try again.

No better.

Of course he wouldn't want me to come over tonight. Of course. It all makes perfect sense, and I will deal with this calmly because this is what I got myself into, and I knew going into this that *complicated* was going to be an understatement.

I am very calmly sick in the toilet, and I wash my mouth out quickly in the sink before anyone catches me, then pop a stick of peppermint gum in my mouth.

Calmly.

Then I head to chem, which is a class I'm in with Kolbie. She's my lab partner.

I sit down at the lab table, brushing my hair back behind my ears and setting out my notebook and pencils on the table. I like the lab, usually. It's a change of pace from normal classes. I get to stand, move. The chemical smell of the classroom is strange and good and it makes me feel like sort of a mad scientist, in control of the whole world.

"Acid rain today, huh?" I say when Kolbie joins me. "Riveting stuff."

She snorts and ties her hair back. "If it were anyone else talking, I'd know they were being sarcastic. But knowing you—"

I smile. Already it feels better than the ones I practiced in the mirror, but still not quite right.

"What's wrong?" she demands. "I'm not pouring any acidy shit in here if you're not on your game." She puts on her safety goggles and makes an X motion with her fingers.

I keep my annoyance off my face. Of course I'm on my game. I'm always on my game. "I'm okay. I swear. I'm just a little overwhelmed."

"Maybe you should calm down every once in a while. Try to relax, and not just with dumb parties. Do something a little more you."

"What do you mean?" I ask suspiciously. What does Kolbie think is a little more *me*? Like, Science Club? Foreign Language Club? Smart People . . . Club?

"Like a book club," she suggests, completely earnest. "Where you read for fun. Or maybe—dating. But, like, just casually."

"Uh-huh."

Kolbie starts inventorying the supplies Mr. Peters has left on our lab table and slides them across to me for double-checking. "pH strips—do you think this is enough? This box is almost empty."

SUCH A GOOD GIRL

"We shouldn't need that many if we don't screw it up."

"And we won't. But anyway—do you remember how I told you I'd hook you up with an older guy?"

"Um, yes. I remember."

"So Jamal is coming to visit this weekend. And he's bringing his best friend since childhood, Sandeep. I have met him. He's really, really cute, and he's super nice. So anyway, I told Jamal that if you were down, we could maybe all go get dinner. Jamal really wants to try the Mexican place downtown if you're into it."

"You did that?"

"Yep." She studies me. "I think we're all good on supplies, don't you?"

I realize I've been running my hands over everything, counting them out for the third time without meaning to. But everything's here: the ammonia, the vinegar, the measuring tools. Everything.

"We're good." I know what I'm doing.

"And this weekend we're good too, right? Unless you have another fund-raiser or scholarship acceptance speech to give?"

I pause.

I think of Alex. I think of his wife.

I think of the way he spoke to me in the classroom today.

I need to do this. I need to be sure I am being a normal high school kid the same way he is pretending to be a normal husband. Besides, maybe Sandeep will be really nice.

Or maybe Alex will notice he's not my only option. He will notice I'm not pining away for him and that I am fine, just fine,

159

just like always. Because I don't make choices I can't handle the ramifications of.

A sharp arrow of pain shoots through my heart. I try smiling again, and it feels strange and mean on my teeth. Weird how hard smiling has gotten lately.

"We're good for this weekend," I echo.

After all, I can always cancel if Alex leaves Jacqueline.

TWENTY-ONE
If

"You look super hot," Neta says. "In fact, I think you should shop in my closet more often." She twirls me in a formfitting red dress with a slightly flared skirt, and I smile. I actually feel pretty good about myself, too.

I try not to think about what Alex would say if he saw me. Would he like the dress? Would he think it was too much?

Kolbie and I are getting ready at Neta's house, because she said she wanted to live vicariously through our dates and was super pissed that Kolbie had not lined up some college-guy action for her.

"Like you couldn't get any without my help," Kolbie sniffed as she put on her eyeliner.

"Which means I needed your help?" I say, a little offended. I'm putting on my makeup by myself. I've gotten a lot better at it in the past few weeks. Of course, I could always do basic makeup, but now I'm rocking the smoky eye.

"Yep," Kolbie says.

"You don't even hesitate, do you?" I grin.

And I let her get away with it. Because she doesn't know better. And she can't know better.

My own secret gives me a little bit of mean satisfaction.

Except this week, I have barely heard from Alex.

Once, in class, I stayed a little late, and all he did was squeeze my hand and say, "Soon." But other than that, it's like we don't even know each other anymore, except as a student and teacher.

My e-mail inbox has stayed empty, although I did send him one. A simple question mark.

?

And nothing else.

But I am not pathetic. I do not stalk. I'm not going to show him how much he's hurting me.

After all, I'm *fine*.

I'm not hurt.

He said he was leaving his wife and that he didn't mind that I wasn't ready for sex, but it's fine. It's all fine.

And that's why I'm still doing this double-date thing with Kolbie and Sandeep.

"Try this, Riley," Neta said, thrusting a lipstick at me. "It'll match perfectly with your dress. Very va-va-voom."

SUCH A GOOD GIRL

"First of all, no one has actually said 'va-va-voom' since, like, the nineties. Secondly, I think that is just a little much for me. But thank you. The red dress is perfect, honestly." I smooth it down over my body. It really is. Neta and I are sort of the same size—except she's all curves where I'm more athletic.

Neta pouts. "Well, put it in your purse in case you're feeling sassy. Just be sure you don't get any on your teeth, okay? Mirror application *only*. Regular checks required."

"Promise." I find my black patent-leather clutch and let her slip the lipstick inside, even though I'm already committed to using the same clear gloss I always do. I already swept on a dramatic eye. The red lip would just seem like too much. I wouldn't even feel like Riley.

Although maybe that would be a good thing.

Kolbie, who is dressed in a flowy dark purple top and leather leggings, finishes her mascara. "Are you ready, Ri? The guys have been downstairs for ten minutes."

"We're late?" I ask. "Should one of us have gone downstairs or something?"

Neta giggles. "No, Ri. It's good for the guys to wait a little bit. Take your time, okay?"

Neta's right. The guys aren't even mad. Sandeep sees me and immediately kisses my hand, like we're in an old movie. "Riley, right?" he asks. "You're just as beautiful as Jamal promised."

I don't even blush, and Sandeep is actually really handsome—he has neatly cut dark hair, a sharp, strong jawline, and lovely eyes. "You're not terrible yourself."

163

He leans in conspiratorially. "New T-shirt," he confesses, and I laugh, because he's actually dressed in a crisp light purple button-up. "Shall we?" he asks. "I hear we're dining at a restaurant place where you actually have to *pay* for the chips and salsa. Very high-class stuff."

I take the arm he's offering, and we walk out to the car with Jamal and Kolbie, who are already kissing and cuddling. We let them have the front seat, and we climb into the back together.

"I have to tell you something," I tell Sandeep. "Something important."

"What?"

"The chips and salsa are free."

"Damn it. Are you telling me I could have worn an actual T-shirt?"

I nod solemnly. "Probably an old one. With a hole, even."

"Well, I have to be honest, then. I was trying to impress you. How am I doing?"

I tilt my hand, giving him the so-so sign. "You'll have to order guacamole. And then we'll see."

He laughs, and the sound is rich and kind. "You're funny, Riley Stone."

And I like Sandeep. When we arrive at the restaurant, he walks around the car and opens my door. And he actually pulls out my chair for me.

"Isn't he great?" Kolbie whispers in my ear as Sandeep orders extra guacamole.

And he is.

SUCH A GOOD GIRL

If my heart weren't all tied up in someone else, I'd really like him.

"What's your major?" I ask him.

"Engineering," he says.

"That sounds like a smart-kid major."

"It is," Jamal interrupts.

"It's Jamal's major too." Kolbie runs her hand over his chest. "His dad was an engineering major, and now he owns a construction company."

"And you?" I ask Sandeep. I grab a chip and opt for salsa instead of guacamole—just for this one.

"When I was little, I wanted to design the rockets that go into space. And I found out you had to have an engineering degree to do that, so I sort of just decided to get one." He shrugs. "So maybe someday I'll move to Texas or Alabama and work for NASA. And my rockets will be in space."

"That's pretty cool, actually," Kolbie says.

"Hey," Jamal interjects. "Mine is cool too. I'm going to take over the family business."

Kolbie leans her head on his shoulder. "I know. And you're going to build us a big house to live in, aren't you?"

Jamal runs a hand through her hair. "The biggest. With a pool and a tennis court."

"I love tennis," Kolbie says, leaning in for a kiss.

"I know you guys are relationship goals right now, but it's a little gross sometimes," Sandeep says, and I laugh.

The waitress comes to take our orders. I get fajitas, and Sandeep orders enchiladas.

165

And extra guacamole.

"Dude," Jamal says. "You have a problem."

Sandeep winks at me.

He's proving a point.

We all talk, and Sandeep slips an arm around the back of my chair. His hand brushes the bare skin of my arm, and I lean into it. I don't pull away.

My phone vibrates, but I ignore it.

"Don't look now," Kolbie says, "but our illustrious French teacher is here with his lovely wife." She giggles. "He must have heard me telling Sara about our double date when I was in class earlier and totally followed us."

My heart drops, but I force myself to giggle too. She thinks she's joking. "A teacher, outside of his natural habitat?" I force a laugh. "I didn't know they were allowed."

"Do I have something to be worried about?" Jamal asks, puffing out his chest.

Kolbie puts her hand on his cheek. "Of course not, baby. I like *older* men. Not old men." She kisses him again for emphasis, and I almost want to scoff. I happen to know Kolbie thinks Alex is more attractive than Jamal.

Pretending that I'm just flipping my hair, I turn my head—and there he is, sitting next to Jacqueline, at a table with maybe five others. His arm is looped around the back of her chair.

He catches my eye, but turns away quickly. I scoot my chair a little closer to Sandeep, but my heart is burning.

So much for him leaving his wife.

166

SUCH A GOOD GIRL

He's just a liar.

Which is fine. Just fine. I don't care.

Funny how much I've been telling myself that lately.

Because it hurts, deep inside me, like I've never quite had anything hurt before, and suddenly I want to be alone. But I can't do that. I can't let him ruin me like that.

When Sandeep excuses himself to go to the restroom, I pick up my phone, and finally, there's an e-mail.

Don't. Please. Don't.

What a joke. I glance back across the restaurant, and anger joins the hot jealousy burning in my chest. He's looking at me again, and his arm is unhooked from the back of her chair.

Then you don't, I type back. I look pointedly at Jacqueline, who is smiling and chatting with the rest of the table, oblivious.

"I don't think I like that guy." Jamal's still staring over at Alex's table. "He keeps looking down here. Gives me the creeps."

Kolbie snuggles into the crook of his arm. "Baby, you're being crazy. He's a weirdo teacher with a forever-young complex. Now, are you going to order me fried ice cream for dessert?"

Sandeep returns to the table and smiles at me. He's so handsome and sweet. "Do you want dessert?" he asks, noticing the open menu.

"Only if we share it," I say, trying to recapture the fun I was having before, but I feel Alex's stare on my bare shoulders.

The waitress comes back and we order two fried ice creams, and Sandeep feeds me little bites on a spoon, which makes me laugh. I feed him bites too, and one falls on his pants because my hand is shaking. He picks it off with his fingers and eats it anyway.

167

Sandeep thinks I am shaking because our situation is funny. But it's not anymore.

"Do you want to take a walk with me?" Sandeep asks when the bill comes. He pays it without asking, which is gentlemanly and sweet, and we don't have to do an awkward tug-of-war with the bill.

I don't let myself glance back at Alex. "Yeah. That sounds really—really nice."

He takes my hand and we walk out of the restaurant while Kolbie and Jamal are still eating ice cream at the table. I half hope Alex sees. I am no desperate girl. I am beautiful. I am desirable. I am not pining away in a puddle of tears while he goes home and makes love to the beautiful, empty wife he told me it was over with.

"I had fun," Sandeep tells me when we get outside. The night is cold, and the sky is cloudless. The moon is big, and nearly full, but the streetlights have washed away most of the starlight. I pull my coat tight around me, and the slight wind raises goose bumps on my legs.

"Me too. You're pretty cool."

He grins. "So are you. I have to admit, I was expecting someone who wanted to get drunk and party all the time. Not that there's anything wrong with that," he amends quickly. "It's just not my thing."

I sigh dramatically and put the back of my hand to my forehead. "Maybe I'm just not there yet, Sandeep."

"Work hard, and one day you will be." His voice is mock-serious. "Listen, I want to give you my number, if that's okay." He hands me a napkin from the restaurant, folded up neatly, which I stick in my coat pocket.

SUCH A GOOD GIRL

"Thanks," I say. "I'll text you."

And then we sort of get quiet.

We stop just under a streetlight. The stoplight under the corner casts his face red. Yellow. Green. "Do you think . . . can I kiss you?" Sandeep asks. He touches my cheek, tentatively, and his fingertips are cold.

I hesitate. "Um. Okay."

He leans in, and I lean in.

And then suddenly, all I can think of is Alex.

Please. Don't. Please.

I can't do this. I'm in too deep.

I pull away, and put my hands on Sandeep's shoulders. "I'm sorry," I tell him. "I'm so sorry. I just can't. Not yet. I'm, um, not feeling well."

And I leave him, on the corner in the streetlight, and hail a taxi to take me home. I text Kolbie that I got sick.

And I pull the napkin out of my pocket while I'm in the cab and I text Sandeep.

I'm so sorry. I had fun, but I'm just not ready.

I wish for a second I had never met Alex, because Sandeep is perfect for me: handsome and sweet and just a touch nerdy. But it's too late for that. I send one final e-mail, just after the cab drops me off in front of my house.

Keep your promise or I'll keep it for you.

He'll know what it means: get rid of Jacqueline, or I will.

169

TWENTY-TWO
Perfect

"Overall, I'm really pleased with this assignment," Alex—Mr. Belrose says as he passes the papers back. "There were a few of you who struggled, but I think that was probably more due to behavioral issues than anything else. Still, if any of you would like to see me after class, I'd welcome the opportunity to talk through your assignments."

We had submitted papers based on the first ten chapters of *Les Mis.* I know mine rocked, naturally. I have this whole Jean Valjean thing down pat. In fact, if we were ever to perform the play, they'd have to cast me as a lead. There would be no question, honestly.

I am more interested in my cuticles than my paper when Belrose tosses it down on my desk. The whole class, I haven't been

SUCH A GOOD GIRL

making eye contact with him. It's his move, really. If he wants me, he knows what to do.

Rob Samuels, who conveniently moved from the back row to the seat next to me since I've sort of been avoiding him, gives a low whistle. "Damn, Stone. Slipping a little, huh?" He grins at me, and I automatically smile back.

We all know I don't slip.

Rob reaches out, and his hand grazes mine. Normally, I pull away when Rob does things like this, but today, I leave my hand where it is, letting Belrose see that Rob likes me too. That Rob has always liked me, and no matter how hard Belrose tries, he will never go back as far as Rob and I do.

He doesn't need to know that Rob isn't a real possibility for me.

"Are you okay, Riley?" Rob asks, his voice soft.

"Excuse me?"

He leans over and nudges my *Les Mis* paper with a knuckle.

I look down, and then do a double take.

What?

That's not possible.

Scrawled hurriedly across the top of the page is not the A I am so used to seeing in Belrose's handwriting. It's not even a B, or God forbid, a C.

It's an F.

On what I happen to know for a fact is a goddamned good paper.

"It's a joke," I tell Rob, but I flip through the other pages for comments. And there are none. Not one. And on a paper that

171

warrants an F, there should at least be another red mark or two that explains *why*.

And the absence of said red marks can only mean one thing: Belrose is screwing with me. He's punishing me for Sandeep. He thinks he has the power here. But he doesn't.

Oh, he doesn't.

I look up at him and for the first time all class I meet his eyes, and I smile.

Challenge accepted.

I take my phone out of my backpack, preparing to send him a scathing e-mail, but Belrose yanks my phone out of my hand roughly.

"You know the rules, Miss Stone." His voice is cold, and he shakes my phone at me. His eyes hold mine, and they're hard. "If you want your phone back, you'll have to come see me after school."

The class is silent. And they should be. They're stunned. They've never seen Belrose be such an asshole. Especially not to a prize pupil like me.

"Fine," I say.

"After school, Stone," he repeats, and starts scrawling on the board.

So this is how he's going to get me to talk to him. Huh. He's going to embarrass me.

Is this his way of getting back at me? Or his weird way of saying he misses me?

I narrow my eyes. Either way, he has no idea who he's playing with.

TWENTY-THREE
Extracurricular

"Mr. Belrose."

I stand in the doorway to his classroom. We don't have cheerleading practice tonight, which is good, because I had to wait some time before all the girls who pretended to need help with their French homework cleared out of his classroom. It's almost four.

"Miss Stone. Please come in. Close the door."

I obey. I want to slam the door, but I know from experience the reverberation will rattle every classroom in the hallway and possibly break the thin glass paneling that exists so teachers *can* close said doors, so I close it softly. "I don't suppose I can have my phone back now."

He draws it out of his pocket, actually looking a little sheepish.

"Here. Um, also, you got an A on your paper. It's in the grade book."

I don't let him see that I was concerned. "I thought so," I say, keeping my voice stiff and professional. "Thank you for your time, Mr. Belrose. I'll keep my cell phone in my backpack in the future."

I'm almost to the door when he speaks again.

"I know you aren't serious with Sandeep."

Ah.

That means he somehow unlocked my phone.

And went through my text messages.

I turn back toward him and watch him from across the room. Rage rises up in my chest. So he can confiscate my phone and just—go through it? What gives him the right?

"Is that so?" My voice shakes, just slightly. I hate it.

"It is." He comes toward me, and I step away from the door.

"And what gives you the right to go through my phone without permission?" I ask, and he's advancing and I'm backing away and then all of a sudden I'm in the corner of the classroom with my back against the wall and he's looming over me.

The blinds on the wall are closed.

No one can see us.

"You've been ignoring me," he says, breathing hard. "I had to do something. You were being impossible."

I can't stand it. I hit him.

But before I can make contact, he catches my arm. "That's not nice, Riley," he says, and pushes my arm up against the wall. He captures the other, too.

SUCH A GOOD GIRL

And then he kisses me. He kisses me softly at first, and even though I hate myself, I kiss him back.

Soft.

Slow.

And then harder, and with more urgency.

He lets me go, finally, breathing hard. "I still care about you, Riley. I'm just taking care of some shit, okay?" His hand is behind my neck, cradling my head away from the cinder blocks that make up the wall. "The house will be empty tomorrow, so just come over if you can."

He releases me like he can barely stand it.

"I'm not just going to be your slut for when your wife isn't around," I tell him. "I thought it was over with her."

"It is," he says. "I swear to God."

I look into his eyes, and reach up to touch his cheek. "It better be," I whisper. "Because you don't want to find out what I'd do if you're playing me."

TWENTY-FOUR
Blood

"I cooked," Alex says. "I hope you're happy."

He's been waiting for me in the den, one leg propped up on the other, his foot wiggling. It's been raining since about five, so I take my boots off and leave them by the door. I couldn't skip cheer tonight. And I wouldn't. If he wants to be treated as a priority, he needs to show me I'm one too.

"What did you make?"

"Lasagna. My grandfather's recipe. And garlic bread." His voice has an edge to it. "It's been ready. I've been waiting." He doesn't stand. Just sits there and stares at me.

"I had practice. You know that. I can't just skip. People

SUCH A GOOD GIRL

would talk." I slip out of my jacket and hang it on the back of a chair. I took a quick shower in the locker room even though I hate the floors in there and there is an actual risk I'm going to get a raging case of athlete's foot. He should be grateful I got here this early.

Alex finally pushes off of the couch and takes my hand, leading me into the kitchen. "You're wearing the necklace," he says, and blood rushes to my cheeks.

"Yes."

I don't tell him I haven't taken it off. I'd almost unclasped it a hundred times, but I never had.

"You hungry?"

"Yes."

It's a lie. I'm not hungry. I'm nervous. He's acting weird— whether it's because he thinks Jacqueline will catch us or he's angry with me or he thinks this whole thing is a stupid mistake, I don't know.

I start to sit down, but before I can, he grabs me. His hands are rough, and he doesn't start gentle with me, like he normally does. He kisses me, hard, his teeth biting into my lips and his hands pushing up roughly under my shirt. I return the kiss, but he grows rougher, and before I know it we're on the kitchen floor and suddenly kissing him isn't fun anymore and I taste blood in my mouth.

I turn my head and shove him away. "Stop!" I push at him and climb to my feet. "What are you doing?"

177

He climbs to his knees. "I'm—I'm sorry, Riley. I just—I wanted you. I missed you." He runs both hands through his hair. "I didn't mean to scare you like that."

"You didn't scare me," I say. "I'm just not some whore you can screw on your kitchen floor, okay?" I pull myself into the chair. "We're not like that."

"Shit. I'm so sorry, Riley. I just missed you so much. It hasn't been easy to be without you." He ducks his head. He still needs a haircut. Parts of his hair, usually messy in a boyish way, are sticking up oddly, making him look a bit crazed. I want to smooth it down, but I restrain myself.

"Could have fooled me," I snap. I touch my lip to see if I'm bleeding, and my finger comes away with a small red spot of blood. "You've been acting like I don't exist."

He pulls himself up. "I—I just had to figure everything out, Riley. I didn't expect Jacqueline to come back. I thought it was over. I thought she was gone. And then all of a sudden she was back, acting like everything was okay and normal, and I was suddenly supposed to act like that too, and I just panicked and I'm sorry. Nothing about my feelings for you have changed. Nothing about our plans have changed. And I haven't touched her." He holds up his hands. "I swear, Riley."

"Well," I say, my fingers sliding over the silverware he's set out for me. They pause on the knife. "I'm not sleeping with you until you get rid of her. I'm not that kind of girl."

His eyes flash. "I never said you were."

I shrug, and I feel like the space below my collarbone is hollow.

SUCH A GOOD GIRL

"Okay," he says. "I will, so long as you never go on another stupid date while we're together."

"Fine." My words are sharp and they hurt even before they leave my tongue.

"Fine. Should we shake on it?"

I stare at him for a moment.

I need something more. Something bigger than a handshake. Something to make him remember who is really in charge.

"No," I say. I stand up and walk to his kitchen counter. "Take off your shirt."

Behind me, I hear the sounds of fabric as he slips it off. I take mine off and drop it behind me. His breathing quickens audibly.

I pull a sharp silver knife from the wooden block on his countertop. It comes free with a *snick*. I turn it this way and that to catch the light from the kitchen fixture.

Alex's eyes widen, but he doesn't step away.

I draw it across my chest in a neat line, opening a short, shallow cut over my heart. The flesh opens more easily than I'd imagine. The blood wells and collects and falls down my chest in well-ordered lines.

I hold it out to him, handle first, the blade resting loosely in my palm.

He stares at the blade for a moment, then takes it from me. He grits his teeth and makes an identical cut just over his own heart, and then grabs me and hold me tight against him. I feel the warmth of his blood against my skin, and for a moment I am angry and hurt and want to give in to him completely all at the same time.

179

AMANDA K. MORGAN

"I promise." He looks down into my eyes.

"Me too." I don't blink.

"It's a blood bond, then. Unbreakable."

"It's forever," I tell him. I close my hand over his on the hilt of the knife.

Things to Know About Riley Stone:

- At age fourteen, Riley founded the Senior Friends Program through her church youth group. The group paired middle- and high-school-aged students with nursing home residents for companionship and fun. The group still thrives today.
- At age fifteen, Riley taught herself to read Braille in her spare time after volunteering at a camp for blind youth.
- Also at age fifteen, Riley briefly reentered therapy, but voluntarily quit after she realized she felt more intelligent than the therapist, attributing most of her issues to being overly type A.
- Her parents eagerly agreed with her self-diagnosis.
- Riley has standing prescriptions that she can call in for, however, and a therapist who will see her when needed. Of course, Riley thinks this is all quite amusing, as she has personally diagnosed at least twelve other people at her school who need therapy more than she does, one of whom is a teacher.

TWENTY-FIVE
Original

"So I heard you hit it off with Sandeep." Neta and I are in art, and she's pulling on her pink bubble gum with her fingers, which is something I really, really find disgusting, but I try not to bug her about. She does this thing where she pulls on it and wraps it around her fingers and then *chews* it again, then basically repeats the whole process, which is frankly just unsanitary.

"How are your watercolors going, girls?" Mr. Wellingsby, the art teacher, stops by our desk, wiggling his long-fingered hands at us inquisitively. He is a total bohem—he's very thin, with flowy, colorful clothes, and he's always talking about seeing love and pain and energy in art and going on about how we can channel our feelings.

AMANDA K. MORGAN

"I'm conceptualizing." Neta grins up at him and pops her gum.

I don't respond. I've actually got a pretty good watercolor going. It's a waterfall. Which means about as much to me as a goldfish. Or a red Converse sneaker.

Or nothing.

"Let your mind flow," he advises, opening his arms as if guiding Neta's creative energies personally. "Riley! I see so much inner turmoil in this picture! Gorgeous!"

I nod seriously. I know exactly how to deal with Mr. Wellingsby. "I'm glad you picked up on that. I really wanted it to show what I'm going through."

He strokes his goatee with his arachnid hands. "I get it. I do. Do you want to talk to the class about it when you're finished?"

I shake my head, keeping my face calm. "I want my art to speak for me. Please."

He touches his head and then extends his finger in an arc. "Yes, Riley. Yes."

And then he sort of wanders off to the next table, managing to look really high and sort of lost. Which he probably is.

He's strangely a great teacher, if you can get past his muddled exterior.

"So Sandeep," Neta reminds me. "Is he the cause of your inner turmoil?"

I snicker. "Oh yes. I'm definitely pining away for him. I think of him day and night. I write long letters for him and send them by the Postal Service. I got his name tattooed on my left breast."

I think of the cut on my chest where my fake tattoo is, and

184

SUCH A GOOD GIRL

feel the corner of my mouth pulls up. If she only knew.

"Then why did Kolbie say you blew him off?" Neta is still messing with her stupid gum. I want to grab it from her and throw it across the room, only I don't actually want to touch it.

"Because I guess I did."

"And why would that be? If you were having a good time, why'd you ditch him?"

For a moment, I resent her. I resent my gorgeous, gum-snapping friend. I want to tell her to leave me alone. But if the tables were turned, would I ask the same question?

Yes.

I bend over my watercolor. "Please don't be mad at me, Neta."

She sighs heavily, the air whooshing out of her lungs, and finally, she stops playing with her gum and drops her hands. "I'm not mad. I just—I don't get it. If you liked him, what the hell?"

"I was scared, okay? And I'm not ready. If I get into something, I give up a lot of other things. And maybe in college I'll be ready to actually be with someone for real, and yeah, Sandeep is almost perfect, but right now, I'm just not."

Neta just sort of looks at me. "You don't have to do anything you don't want to do, Ri."

I paint green into my waterfall so I don't have to meet her eyes, which I know without looking are too kind right now. "I know."

"Hey," she says. "Look." She points across the room.

I follow her finger. "Um, what?" I see Anthony Waterford, half asleep on his arm, in the corner.

185

"No. Look at Kamea."

I glance at Kamea, who I sort of don't like, just on principle. It's not because she's a bad person or anything. Because she's not. And not because she's particularly irritating.

Of course, it's not like she's *great*, either. She dresses almost exactly the same, every single day, in these stupid button-up cardigans. Her closet probably looks like a cartoon character's closet, with just the exact same outfit, over and over and over and over. She couldn't get more boring if she made an actual effort.

And of course she's this cute, perky little girl-next-door type of blonde who is basically built to look good in any type of clothes. You know, the ones who fit into everything when you go shopping together and then look amazing in it?

Kamea has that body.

But she wears the same stupid cardigans.

And on top of that, she has one of those *voices*. Those high-pitched baby voices that belong on a girl, like, ten years younger that of course guys find attractive but is actually sort of disgusting.

And Neta and Kolbie both like her.

And she has been in second place for valedictorian for as long as I can remember.

"Look at the necklace," Neta prods.

My eyes drop to the gold chain around her neck, and my throat tightens.

Oh my God.

Holy shit.

A little wooden chess piece hangs from the chain.

SUCH A GOOD GIRL

A little wooden king that doesn't look one-of-a-kind at all.

"You and Kamea must shop at the same store." Neta giggles. "Awkward."

I don't answer her. My fist closes around my own necklace and I'm pulling on the chain until it digs into the back of my neck. And somewhere, deep in the recesses of my mind, I'm imagining pulling the necklace tight around Kamea's neck until her eyes bug out. And she doesn't even struggle. She just stares at me, like she does in class when she doesn't know an answer, like maybe, just maybe, I'll help her.

Because it looks like maybe, just maybe, Kamea's also getting a little French tutoring on the side.

"Don't freak out, Ri. It definitely looks better on you."

I whip my head back to Neta. "I'm not worried."

But I know that Alex has a free period not next period—but the period after.

And when he does, I march directly into his classroom and close the door, my arms behind my back.

"Hello, lovely." He touches the space above his heart where he cut himself. Mine barely stings anymore. I have two Band-Aids over my cut and I've religiously applied Neosporin. A blood bond is one thing, but I don't want a scar.

Inside, my temper rages, but I force myself to look at Alex. To study him. I thought he was smarter than this. I thought he would know better than to try to play two of us.

Especially when I'm one of them.

His eyebrows lower slightly. He's figuring it out. He rises from

187

his desk. "What's wrong, Riley?" he asks, coming toward me. "Is everything okay?"

He doesn't touch me like he did last time we were alone in his classroom. That is a wise decision. I am not sure I could handle his skin. I would melt or I would attack. I am not sure which.

I put myself at risk for him, and he doesn't even care.

"Kamea Myers," I say, my voice a whisper.

"Pardon me?"

"Kamea Myers." I repeat myself. I look at him.

There is no response. Absolutely nothing. His face doesn't color. He doesn't look at his shoes. His eyes are trained on mine. "I don't understand, Riley. Would you mind catching me up here?" Finally, his eyes take on a small note of panic. "She doesn't . . . know about us, does she?"

Very slowly, I unhook the little necklace from around my neck. I hold it out to him, the chess piece swinging back and forth, hypnotic.

"This is what I'm talking about, Alex. This."

"Your necklace?"

His face is still a canvas of questions and innocence. He's good.

"She has the exact same necklace, Alex." I crush his name between my teeth, grinding out the two syllables. "Now, do you want to tell me how that's possible? Has she been getting extra French tips on the side, maybe? Some private lessons?"

He shakes his head, finally breaking eye contact. "No. Absolutely not. And that's impossible. The man . . . he told me those necklaces were one of a kind. She couldn't have one. It doesn't make sense." He lets out his breath, then looks at me again. "I swear on my life—

SUCH A GOOD GIRL

on *your* life—that I didn't give her a necklace, Riley. I never would. That's not her. That's you and me. That's us, okay?"

He doesn't blink.

"Huh," I say.

"Trust me, Riley. I've never felt about anyone like I feel about you. Please, please, just trust me on this, okay?"

I don't.

Trust him.

And he's pleading.

His eyes stray now, from me to the window behind me, to make sure what we're doing looks PC. But he's desperate for me to believe him. Desperate. He looks disheveled, somehow, not the in-control teacher who I stopped by to see.

"Okay." The word I give him is tight and brittle and already splintering around the edges. "Fine."

His face relaxes.

I turn toward the door to leave him. I suddenly just want to go back to class.

"I'm leaving Jacqueline tonight."

It bursts out of him. I pause with my hand on the door, and I turn back to him. "Make sure you do. I'm not a mistress."

And then, without waiting for him to say another word, I walk back to class.

I don't even look back to see if he's watching me.

I know he is. Just like always.

It doesn't cross my mind that I might have underestimated him.

TWENTY-SIX
Mobile

There was a password on my iPhone, but it appears Alex knew it.

He knew *I knew* that he knew.

I lay in bed, staring at my ceiling, my cell phone resting on my chest.

My mom would yell at me for that. She says you can get cancer that way, by keeping your phone too close to your body.

I don't know why I'm even thinking about that right now.

Not after what just happened.

Not after what I just found.

I stare at it. I imagine it jumping with my heartbeat. I imagine it starting on fire so I never, ever have to find out.

Alex left me something on my phone.

SUCH A GOOD GIRL

Something in a photo album. One that I don't recognize. One that I don't remember being on there before Alex took my phone away from me. One that is titled *FORRILEY*.

A photo album that I definitely have never, ever seen before.

The first picture is the album—the thumbnail—and it's blurred. I can't tell what it is. No matter how long I look at it.

But it's the color of skin.

I close my eyes slowly and then reopen them, focusing on the ceiling. What did he take pictures of while he was sitting at his desk all day? Am I even ready to see this?

Is this going to be gross?

No. Alex isn't like that.

I bite down on the inside of my bottom lip.

I click the album open.

The first photo is the blurred photo.

And the second photo is of me. Asleep. My right hand is tucked under my head, and my hair is wild, like I've been tossing and turning. My legs are tangled in the sheets.

My sheets.

In my bed.

Oh my God.

I flip through the rest of the pictures quickly. It's all me, in my white tank top and pajama pants, in various positions as I slept. In some, my arms are splayed out. In some, my top has ridden up, showing my stomach. In others, I've barely moved in my bed.

My bed.

In my own house.

Alex didn't take any pictures when he confiscated my phone during class. He broke into my house when I was sleeping and took pictures of me with my own phone.

And somehow, I had *no idea.*

Why would Alex do that? Why wouldn't he tell me he was there, or wake me up? Why would he chance getting caught sneaking into my room?

I think of Alex in my room at night, watching me, and my heart feels strange and scared and angry and excited, all at once. What is this, though? Is this some sort of insurance? Is Alex trying to *scare* me?

This is not normal boyfriend behavior. Even a girl who has never actually dated knows that.

It's been three days since he told me he was going to break it off with Jacqueline. Three days. And he hasn't done it. Jacqueline's teal-blue car is still parked out in front of their curb every single day, and every single day Alex tells me the same exact thing: *Soon. I swear. I love you.*

I tell him that I love him back, but a little hate seeps in around the corners. And then I let him go home to Jacqueline.

My room is strangely cold, but I don't want to go down the hall to check the thermostat. I just want to lay here. My heart hurts in my chest in a way that has become strange and familiar all at once.

And I think of Alex, standing over me while I slept, my phone in his hands.

My phone buzzes, turning the screen from my strange sleeping photos to Kolbie, smiling sweetly at the camera, her hands behind

SUCH A GOOD GIRL

her back. I want to turn her off, to be wholly alone, but I force myself to answer.

"Hey, girl." I try to sound visibly cheerful, but I feel strange. My skin feels odd, like it's falling asleep over my muscles.

"Don't 'hey, girl' at me, Riley. Why haven't you been answering your phone?" Her tone is definitely Pissed Kolbie. I've heard her this way before, but never at me.

I cringe and hold the phone about an inch away from my ear. "Uh, what?"

"How many times did I call you? Don't you think maybe your friends need you? Or are you too caught up in Ri-Ri land to care?"

"I . . . don't know," I finish, because it's the truth. I suppose I noticed they'd called some, but I actually went home early on Friday and I've spent most of the weekend studying and organizing, with thoughts of Alex crawling around in the back of my head. Which was stupid. I always swore I'd never be one of those girls. And maybe, just maybe, I hadn't checked my messages all weekend. I pull my covers over my head but keep my phone to my ear. I deserve to hear her out. I know it.

"Well, you're being a shit friend, Riley, because first you walked out on Sandeep, and you wouldn't even talk to me about it."

"Yeah, well, I panicked, okay? I don't want him to get in the way of my priorities. I'm sorry." My words are defensive.

"I know, Riley, but if you were just going to ghost a good guy, I wouldn't have set you up with Jamal's best friend. You could have at least given him some sort of explanation."

193

"I'm sorry," I say again, and this time I actually do sound properly sorry.

"Just don't expect me to set you up with someone good again until you can actually handle it. Sandeep felt like shit, just so you know. And so did I. He really liked you, Ri." Her voice softens, just slightly. "I'm not saying you had to be with him if you weren't into him. And if he did something weird, you'd tell me, right? I won't be mad. I swear."

"I know. And he didn't. Please don't think that." And I do know. And I like him, too. There's a part of me that wishes I never touched Alex, so this Sandeep thing could happen. I shift beneath my blankets, my legs twisting up in the sheets. What would I be doing now if I hadn't ever gotten involved with Alex? Would I be talking to Sandeep instead of hiding out in my own house, feeling completely ignored and depressed?

"And you haven't answered Neta's calls, either."

"So you guys have been *talking* about me?" My voice is cutting. I can't believe they're hanging out without me, talking behind my back.

Kolbie is quiet for a few seconds, and then: "Well, more about her dead grandmother, but yeah, I guess so. She was worried about you. I was more pissed."

My body turns strange and cold for a half second. "Neta's grandmother died?" I say.

"Yeah."

"But she wasn't sick, was she?"

"No. She had a heart attack. And Neta's been calling you and calling you and so have I, but you haven't been there."

SUCH A GOOD GIRL

I swallow hard.

"Is Neta okay?"

"No."

Kolbie's furious at me. This isn't about Sandeep at all. Of course it's not. It's about Neta and the fact that I'm a completely horrible friend. Why couldn't I just check a text? Or return a call? Or do anything besides be completely stupid and self-involved?

"The funeral's Monday. First Trinity Church. The arrangements are in your texts, if you'd ever care to check them." She says it like I'll probably turn her down—like she expects me to. Like I'm the biggest disappointment ever.

"I'll be there, Kolbie."

"I should think so." Kolbie's voice is thin ice over a winter pond. Brittle and cold and hateful. And I don't fault her for it.

"Listen, Kol—"

But she's not there. She's hung up without saying good-bye.

TWENTY-SEVEN
Undercover

My dad has two pickups. There is one that he drives to work and treats like a baby; he spends his weekends washing it and waxing it and using a special cloth to clean it that he spent, like, thirty bucks on. Then, there's the other truck. The *real* pickup truck, that is actually used for pickup-type things.

He lets my uncle borrow it most of the time. It's faded blue and rusted and he uses it to drag around lawn mowers and hasn't properly cleaned it in almost twenty years. The windows are the kind you have to roll down by hand and they're smeared with years of fingerprints.

And so, the night before Neta's grandmother Pilar's funeral, I tell my dad I need to tote some stuff for the school food drive, and

SUCH A GOOD GIRL

so it doesn't seem weird that I need to borrow the old pickup truck that basically no one ever sees my immediate family or me in, ever.

When I start the rust bucket, it takes two tries for it to catch, but the engine (or whatever) finally shrieks and turns over. I cringe. It's louder than I'd prefer, but it *is* ancient. I think it's actually from the eighties or something, so it's even older than Ethan. But I let it run for a minute, and the noise level evens out.

I start off toward the school, and then I turn in the direction of my destination: Alex's house. I know the way by heart . . . the names of the little streets, which intersections have stoplights and which have four-way stops. The sidewalks and trees and little painted mailboxes in his neighborhood have become almost as ordinary to me as my own street.

I park just down the road, in front of a squatty little orange house with all its lights off, and kill the engine in a spot where I can still see the Belrose home and Jacqueline's cute little teal car parked out in front.

She's still there.

Of course she is.

If he'd told her he wanted a divorce, wouldn't she have fled to her mother's or sister's or something? Isn't that what happens when people ask for divorces? One of them *leaves*?

It's not like I'm stupid. It means he didn't ask. It means he lied. It means nothing has changed and I'm just a fool who is wasting her time.

And I am not a girl to be made a fool of.

I grind my teeth and sink down in the seat. It's twilight, and

197

soon, the streetlights will flicker on, but just now, the sun has sunk to the point where it's hard to see anything, which means no one will be able to see me in my dad's old pickup.

What is taking him so long to leave her? Does he still have feelings for a woman who totters around complaining and reading gossip magazines? Is he that shallow that he would choose her over me?

Yes. Being with Jacqueline is easier, certainly. But there is no way that she could be better.

Cold is beginning to seep in through the car, and I wish I'd brought along a blanket or a thermos of hot cocoa. I button my jacket up to my neck, and the streetlights come on, bathing the Belrose house in a yellow light that I happen to know comes in through the front windows and rests very softly on the beige carpet in the living room.

I blow into my hands and wrap my arms around my body, and then something happens.

The door opens on the familiar little brick house, and two people walk out onto the front steps. There is Alex, in a hoodie and jeans, not dressed enough for the cold of the night, and Jacqueline, in a red peacoat and high heels, a long wool scarf wrapped around her neck. They walk to her little car together, and he leans forward with a sense of familiarity.

They kiss, just for a quick moment, and his hand touches her arm in a way that means she is his.

And then she just drops her purse into the passenger side door, crosses to the other side, and drives away.

SUCH A GOOD GIRL

He waves at her, then walks back into the house, like he has done nothing out of the ordinary.

My fingers dig into the cracking vinyl of the seat.

They *kissed.*

It was not the kiss of a couple that is breaking apart. It was a worn-in, familiar type of kiss, the kind that's repeated for hellos and good-byes and maybe at night before turning out the bedside lamp. Something done out of habit. Not forced. Not unhappy.

He walked outside to see her off.

And then he *kissed* her.

With lips he promised were mine.

My heart rots from the inside out. I feel tears start in my eyes, but I blink them away. I turn the key in the pickup, but it only whimpers in a sad, ragged way. I turn the key again, and the truck groans and screams but finally starts, and in the house I am parked next to, a light goes on and the curtains are switched to the side.

I hit the gas and speed away, not caring, the truck rattling loudly along the little street.

Let them stare.

Alex doesn't care either. Obviously. He's certainly making it very clear he and Jacqueline are still very much a thing and I do not matter.

When I get home, I walk into the house through the mudroom and into the kitchen. Immediately, my mother hugs me. "Baby," she says. "You should have told me what was going on."

I untangle myself from her arms. I can't remember the last time we hugged. "Um, I'm okay. What?"

199

My mind jumps to Alex.

She steps back, leaning against the kitchen island. She looks concerned, for once. The lines around her face look deeper than usual, and her eyes are blurry and tired. Her blond hair, the same shade as mine, seems to have more silver highlights around her crown. "Neta's grandma. The funeral tomorrow. Have you been over there to talk to her? Have you figured everything out?"

"Yes."

That's a lie. I haven't been over there. Neta hasn't answered any of my calls, and her text had simply said, NO THANKS, EVERY-THING FINE. Which was code for LEAVE ME ALONE YOU SELFISH BITCH.

Which is fair.

So I let her know I was here if she needed me and then left her alone. And I texted Kolbie and extended the same offer, and of course she hasn't responded. In fact, she may have blocked me. I'm not sure. I'm scared to try to figure it out.

"That's good, sweetie." My mother reaches out to smooth my hair, then pulls back, as if thinking better of it. She's already hugged me once. That's our family love quota for the year, basically. Two touches in one day would just be ridiculous.

"I got into Princeton," I say, off the cuff, and she smiles at me, sort of sad.

"I know, honey. I remember. You told us at dinner."

Which is just weird, because I know for a fact no one at dinner was listening to me.

I leave her in the kitchen and go back upstairs to be alone, where everything makes just a little more sense. I lay out my black

SUCH A GOOD GIRL

dress with thick black tights and black shoes, and I text Kolbie and Neta to tell them I'll be there, I promise.

And I fall asleep.

But the next day at the church, outside the chapel, things don't make sense either. Because where Kolbie and I should be standing, alongside Neta, there is someone else. Someone with a very similar GPA and a pretty chess-piece necklace.

Kamea Myers.

Standing right in the thick, with Neta and her entire family.

Holding Neta's hand while she cries.

I slip up to Kolbie, who gives me a grateful smile and slides her arms around me, pulling me into a big hug. I am stiff with surprise for a millisecond before I melt into her. I missed her.

"I'm so sorry," I whisper. "I've been going through some stuff, Kolbie, but I know that's no excuse and it's not about me."

She hugs me a little tighter. "I know Riley. I'm sorry I was so hard on you. I know you'd never just ditch us without a good reason." She pulls away, and her eyes are misty.

My whole body feels heavy with the truth. Would Kolbie hate me if I told her? "Yeah." I clear my throat and flick my eyes toward Kamea. Neta hasn't even looked at me. She's just standing there, her pretty shoulders hunched over. "How's she doing?"

Kolbie shakes her head. "Neta's a mess. I don't know how to help her. She's so close to her grandma, you know?"

I nod. Pilar was almost a mother to Neta; she lived with her family. She helped Neta with her homework and dropped her off at school before she got her license.

201

"What's Kamea doing here?" I can't help but ask.

"I don't know. I think Kamea was, like, adopted by her cousin's brother-in-law or something. Some family connection. And they've gotten closer lately. So try not to hate her too much today? Please? I promise you can go back to full hate tomorrow."

"I don't hate anyone," I protest. But my eyes keep straying to the chain around Kamea's neck. And for some reason, the chain I'm wearing under my own dress feels cold. And heavy.

And wrong.

Like maybe I shouldn't be wearing it in a church. Or at a funeral.

Neta finally turns away, releasing Kamea's hand, and comes toward us. Her eyes are, for once, free of the dark makeup she normally wears, and she still looks stunning even though it's obvious she's been crying. She throws her arms around me. "I missed you," she whispers. "Are you okay?"

I stare at her. She's been worried about *me*? "Um, yeah. I'm so sorry I'm been gone. I've been . . . it doesn't matter. Are you okay?"

She wipes at her eyes with the back of her hand. "Sure." She tries to smile, but it's shaky and lasts only for a moment. "Thank you both for being here." She wraps her arms around Kolbie, and tears fall down her cheeks onto Kolbie's sweater. "I don't know what to do."

And I realize I don't know what to say to her. What do you say to someone when a most important part of her life is just . . . gone? "I'm so sorry, Neta. Please let us know . . . what we can do."

The words feel stupid and empty even as I say them, but she tries to smile again and cries even harder, and I just feel silly and lost.

"It's okay," Neta says finally, through her tears, and I feel like

SUCH A GOOD GIRL

she's forgiving me. Her mother, who looks like her slighter older sister, comes to get her from us, and leads her daughter away, and they're buried in each other's arms.

Kolbie swallows hard, trying to keep from crying herself. "This sucks."

I nod. "Yeah."

We head into the church, and the usher seats us two rows back—close to where Neta's family will sit when they come in. Kamea walks up shyly and smiles at us, hesitant. She doesn't look particularly sad.

"Can I sit here?" she asks, looking back and forth between the rows of pews. Apparently she's not family enough to sit with the actual family.

"Sure," I say.

"Yeah," Kolbie choruses.

My eyes stray to her necklace.

I wonder again if she has French poetry readings.

"*Oui,*" I say.

"Huh?" Kamea asks, and wedges into the row right next to me, so she's the very last person in the pew. If we're singing today, we'll have to share a hymnbook.

I just smile like I'm baring my teeth and fan myself with the bulletin I was given when I walked in.

"This is so sad, isn't it?" Kamea whispers. "I feel so bad for Neta."

"Yeah," Kolbie says, and looks at me quizzically. Small talk at funerals isn't really my thing, but if I'm being honest, small talk with Kamea Myers isn't exactly my thing either. Still, I'll be kind, for Neta's sake.

203

"I like your outfit," I tell Kamea as more people file into the church. "It's very pretty." I eye her mauve pencil skirt and jacket combo with a tan silk top beneath. It's definitely probable that the jacket even has shoulder pads. It looks like she went straight to the mom section at Ann Taylor, but I suppose for that section, it's very nice. It probably cost a lot. Of course, I choose *not* to shop in the stores for people over forty, but that's my prerogative.

"Thanks," she says. "I don't wear a lot of black, so I had to buy it special for today."

"The necklace, too?" I ask innocently. My own necklace against my skin. *Why isn't it warming up? It's so hot in here. Why is it so hot in here?* I wave my bulletin faster.

She picks up the little chess piece off of her collarbone. "This?" she asks. "Oh, no. My own grandmother bought this for me from Costco. I know it's a bit silly, but it means a lot to me."

"Costco, huh?" Flames lick around the corners of my heart.

She smiles a little. "No judging! It's from my grandmother. It's special."

"Of course not." I smile at her. "I'm sure it *is* special."

I turn back toward the front of the church as the family is escorted in, my heart a dying lead thing in my chest. Could Kamea be telling the truth? Her grandmother got the necklace from Costco? What does that say about Alex?

"Now, was that so hard?" Kolbie mutters in my ear, her voice barely above a breath.

I want to laugh.

And then I want to turn to Kamea and tear her eyes out.

204

SUCH A GOOD GIRL

But it's a funeral, and I'm a nice girl above all, so I sit still and quiet and listen to the service and say my prayers for Neta and her family and her grandmother's soul.

When we all stand to leave, I stick my foot out and Kamea just happens to trip out into the aisle.

"What is wrong with you?" Kolbie asks.

I look at her, wide-eyed. "Oh my God. That was an accident, I swear."

I step into the aisle and help Kamea up and out of the way of the other mourners. "Are you okay?" I ask. "Did you twist your ankle?"

She shakes her head. "I'm sorry, I didn't realize you were trying to walk. I'm so clumsy."

"It's not your fault. Do you hurt anywhere?"

"I think I'm okay. Seriously, Riley, thank you so much." She is flustered and her tanned cheeks are pink with embarrassment.

I put my hand on her shoulder. "If you're sure, Kamea."

She's sure.

I return to Kolbie, and I wait until I have hugged Neta and her whole family and am alone in my car to Google the necklace.

There is a listing for it at Costco. There is also one at Target, and a very similar one on Amazon.

My lead heart grows heavier.

I type an e-mail to Alex.

I KNOW ABOUT THE NECKLACE AND I KNOW YOU'RE STILL WITH HER.

I send the e-mail in a mad rage.

205

TWENTY-EIGHT
Discussions

The classroom phone rang during Shakespeare.

That in itself was not a rare occurrence.

Nor was the fact that Mrs. Hamilton looked at me and said, "Miss Stone, would you mind stopping by the counselor's office?"

Everyone knows that when I'm summoned to the counselor's office, it's because I've just won another ridiculous scholarship or maybe some representative from some college wants to speak to me, or it's just some generally positive thing. So I leave everything on my desk (how long does it take to say, "Thank you!" and pose for a photo?) and skip down to Ms. Felcher's office to see how I can be of service.

But what I did not expect to see is what I am looking at exactly now, with a very frozen smile on my face.

SUCH A GOOD GIRL

Because my parents are on one side of the desk, with very stock-photography concerned parents looks carefully aligned on their deliberately parental faces. How pleasant of them.

More concerning is that on the other side of the desk is Ms. Felcher, looking a bit surprised (although perhaps she got just a tad too much Restylane at her last appointment) alongside none other than Alex Belrose.

And judging by the rosiness along the tops of his ears and the perfectly even set of his lips, he is angry.

No one could know anything, could they? Wouldn't the principal be here? Wouldn't it all be a bigger deal than just this?

"Hello, Riley," he says, his tone perfectly normal . . . for a teacher.

"Hello, Mr. Belrose. Mom. Dad. Ms. Felcher. To what do I owe the pleasure?" My tone is perfectly normal . . . for a student who has just been surprise-attacked by a meeting with her parents, a teacher (with whom she has zero romantic connection), and the school guidance counselor.

"Well," Miss Felcher says, "please have a seat, Miss Stone."

She has never called me Miss Stone before. Ever.

This is serious.

"There are no extra chairs," I point out.

"Oh!" she says, and runs out into the general office for one of the lumpy green waiting-room chairs, which she drags in slowly, bumping it against either side of her door frame.

Alex doesn't even offer to help her.

She leaves the seat sort of between my parents, but a bit behind,

207

AMANDA K. MORGAN

so that I when I sit down, crossing my legs, I don't exactly feel like I'm part of the whole conversation. I spread out the skirt of my little blue dress neatly around my legs just like nothing is wrong. Nothing at all.

Then I swallow my feelings down in one great lump and try not to throw them up all over my parents.

Ms. Felcher continues, adjusting her cat-eye glasses just a bit. "First of all, we'd like to share that nothing about this meeting will be documented at this point."

Something in my chest loosens, just a bit.

"However."

It tightens again.

"Mr. Belrose has called your mother and father in for a rather unprecedented conference. It seems he is very confused and a bit concerned about your recent academic performance in his class, so he set up this *unannounced* meeting with your parents. Without informing me." She shoots him a look, which he ignores. Instead, he steeples his fingers and looks at my father, then my mother, and finally, me.

"As you know, Riley is a smart girl. The most intelligent, I believe, in the school. Maybe the most intelligent and promising pupil I've ever had."

My father puffs up, like he's never heard this feedback before. "We're very proud of her," he says, and suddenly I'm actually a little embarrassed. Where has he been? Where have either of them been? He glances back at me and pats me awkwardly on the knee, his hand stiff and open.

208

SUCH A GOOD GIRL

What is the point of my entire existence?

"That's why I'm so alarmed right now."

My mother leans forward, both hands clutching her brown Coach handbag. "Excuse me? Concerned? About our Riley?" She shakes her head, like she must be hearing wrong.

"Yes, Mrs. Stone. Very concerned." He produces copies of my recent homework. Homework I know for an absolute fact I aced. Homework that was perfect and flawless and double-checked before I turned it in. He presents it to my parents.

C. D. F. D. F. C minus. D plus.

And of course, neither of my parents nor Ms. Felcher speak French, so there's no use telling them my French teacher is attempting to get back at me for trying to get him to leave his wife. There's no use asking them to check my French.

I am at his mercy.

I glare at Alex across the table and let my parents gasp at the false red marks and clutch at their hearts.

"Riley," my mother says. "What's going on? Is something wrong?"

I scoot to the very edge of my seat and look over at the homework, and flick my eyes up to Alex's face. I hope he's enjoying his little show. He knows he has me trapped. He knows every student likes him. He knows he's won Most Favored Teacher every second since he's been here, and does loads of community service, and is generally held in high regard ever since the *Hartsville News* did a piece on him last year.

And what am I going to say, really?

209

AMANDA K. MORGAN

I look back down at the work. "Funny," I say lightly. "I thought I did a rather good job on these."

Alex peers at me from behind his steepled fingers, unshakable. "It appears you need to take another look then, Riley. I think that might be your problem; perhaps you aren't spending enough time on your homework."

"What do you recommend, Mr. Belrose?" Mom asks, using her Voice of Motherly Concern, the one she hasn't had to get out and dust off since the Ethan days, when parent-teacher-counselor conferences were a lot more frequent (and merited).

Belrose drops his fingers to my papers and moves forward conspiratorially. "Now, I wouldn't normally do this, but as a bad grade for the semester would move Riley out of her valedictorian standing, I'd like to see her just a little more often. Perhaps she should spend some time with me after school, when she doesn't have cheerleading practice. It will, I'm afraid, take a very serious time investment."

"Is cheerleading getting in the way of her studies?" Dad asks.

"I wouldn't pull her out of cheerleading . . . yet." Alex studies me like I'm not even listening, like I'm something in a zoo behind glass instead of a real girl. "But she should be very, very careful."

He's threatening me.

He doesn't want me to stop spending time with him. And he's willing to drag my parents into this mess in order to prove it.

He's willing to ruin my entire future just to keep me.

I feel my pulse quicken, but I don't move.

"Does that sound okay, Miss Stone?" Miss Felcher prods.

210

SUCH A GOOD GIRL

I let a smile spread across my face. "Absolutely, Ms. Felcher."

"Then I think we're done here." Mr. Belrose gathers my papers into a neat stack. "Unless there are any questions." He stands and tucks the papers under his arm.

My dad stands and takes his hand. "Thanks for caring about our daughter this much, Mr. Belrose. You're a good man."

Alex looks at me. "I'm just trying to do the right thing, Mr. Stone."

"Yes, thank you, Mr. Belrose," I say. I stand, straightening my dress.

It's only then that Mr. Belrose allows a flash of an emotion I can't quite identify cross his face, and I let myself smile. If he's going to play dirty, I'll play dirtier.

And that means I'll have to be more perfect than ever.

TWENTY-NINE
Love and Hate

"So you're not angry with me," Alex says for the thirteenth time.

I'm back at his house, and it's 6:42 a.m. I was supposed to meet him at school for an early morning study session, but since Jacqueline just happens to be in Vegas with her girlfriends, I surprised him at home, like I couldn't wait to see him.

"No. I'm not. I understand your reasons."

We're on the couch, and my head is in his lap. His hand strokes my hair slowly, softly, touching each strand like they are fine little woven bits of silk. I feel . . . special. Important.

"Your parents seemed nice," he offers, and I laugh. It's funny, in a weird, strange way, like this whole thing is screwed-up funny, and I don't even know what's going to happen next anymore.

SUCH A GOOD GIRL

And I used to have everything so smoothed out that I knew exactly what my next move was at any given time.

He leans down to kiss the top of my head. "You know I love you, Riley, don't you?" he asks.

I squirm around so my face is up, and he pushes my hair out of my eyes. "I need you to do something for me," I tell him.

"Okay."

"Be mine. One hundred percent mine. For real. I can't keep doing this otherwise."

His hand freezes on my forehead. "I will, Riley. I swear to God I will. I just can't right now. Not yet."

Alex kissing Jacqueline flashes across my mind's eye. "What's the holdup, then?" I try to pitch my voice to sound casual, but it doesn't. I don't. I sound jealous and catty and my voice has a harsh catch in it.

He lets out his breath. "It's just that Jaqueline's life is really hard right now, and I don't want to pile on, you know? As soon as she sorts everything out just a little bit more, I'll be able to talk with her, and we'll separate. Really separate, I mean. I won't let her come back this time."

I feel like someone has just put a vise grip on my heart. "Um, excuse me?"

He starts stroking again, but instead of his hand feeling good on my face, it's annoying me. I push it away and sit up next to him on the couch so I can look at him. "Why is now *not* a good time, exactly?"

He looks uncomfortable. "Well, her Fine Wines group, they're

213

just being really mean to her right now. She's so beautiful, you know, women are always just mean to her, and she doesn't handle it all that well. She needs my help. She's delicate. I'm sure you get it. You're beautiful, too."

"Please don't compare me to her," I say coldly.

"But you understand, right?" He grabs my hands and holds them tightly in his.

I study his face. The wide jawline, the stubble, the deep green eyes, and I realize, on some level, I hate him a little bit. I hate the man who made me all the promises in the world and just won't keep them.

And I love him.

But I do hate him.

He leans in, slowly, closing his eyes, and I let him kiss me anyway. The kiss is slow and good, just like all of his kisses, and I hate myself a little too, for letting him kiss me like that. He starts lifting my shirt, but I pull away.

"You know the rules." I tap him lightly on the nose. "Is she gone?"

"For the weekend." He sulks, and I laugh because I know I'm supposed to give in, but I don't. "She's very depressed. I'm just worried about her. Really worried." He looks down.

I cock my head to the side. Is he confessing to me that he's worried about his wife? His wife who he said he wants to leave?

Does he want me to be *sympathetic*?

On what level is this—any of this—okay?

I fight the manic laugh trapped in my throat.

SUCH A GOOD GIRL

"We're been married for almost six months, Riley. I care about her."

Suddenly, I don't feel like I'm a part of him anymore. I feel like I'm in another room, or another house, and something's separating us. Maybe a curtain, or a window screen, or maybe I'm watching a fuzzy film of someone I used to know but don't quite anymore, and the communication is delayed, like I can see his lips moving but the meaning doesn't hit me until just a moment later.

"I'm so glad you understand me," he says gratefully.

He's wrong.

I don't understand him.

And clearly, he thinks I'm an idiot if he thinks I'm going to stand by and let me be a little pawn in his sick game.

Rage squeezes my heart. The veins burst and blood spurts and I die inside.

If Jacqueline were to just disappear, maybe it wouldn't be so weird. She is depressed, after all. And she is in the way. Of us. Of happiness. And she's clearly a horrible person.

If only I were a killer.

I squeeze Alex's hands. "I understand," I tell him. I touch his face softly. Kindly. I am there for him, he thinks. I am his silly little waiting-around toy.

"Can I see you tonight?" he asks, his voice low and gravelly, and I know he is dying to get his hands on me. They drop to my waist and squeeze, and I wiggle away and sling my backpack over my shoulders.

"Thanks to your surprise meeting with my lovely parents, I

215

definitely can't get out of any more cheerleading practices or study sessions or anything without looking suspicious." I kiss him lightly, but he furrows his brow.

"Huh? *My* meeting?"

I run my hands along his hairline and behind his ears. "Don't be ridiculous, Alex."

"I didn't schedule that meeting."

I smile. He wants to play. How cute.

I'm just not in the mood.

"I'll see you at school, okay, Alex?"

I lean over and kiss him one more time, hard and fast, and his hands are everywhere they shouldn't be, so I untangle myself.

"You need to be there soon yourself," I warn him. "And don't mess up my hair."

And then I walk out the back door into the cold morning sunlight. A few snowflakes are falling from the sparse cloud cover, and I smile into the odd weather and put on my hat before walking through the back gate into the alley.

Alex Belrose is going to be all mine, one way or another.

I am sure of it.

Things to Know About Riley Stone:

- When Riley Stone learned about the water crisis in Michigan, she began selling water bottles with the #HARTSVILLECARES hashtag–and ending up raising more than five thousand dollars. She spent the money on bottled water, which she sent to the impacted areas.

- Riley also began an anonymous gossip newsletter for the high school and employed her fellow students as models for the advertisements. The publication was eventually shut down by the school, but no one ever found out Riley ran the newsletter, and Riley made out with fifteen hundred dollars in profit, even after paying her models (who *did* get detention).

- Last year, Riley started a letter-writing campaign for the troops overseas. The effort gained statewide attention, and Riley ended up sending more than ten thousand letters and five hundred carefully selected care packages. She assembled a team of community volunteers and has since received multiple requests to run the campaign annually.

- At age fourteen, Riley's algebra teacher, Mrs. Corkstone, became very interested in her. While Riley passed her class with an A plus (as usual), Mrs. Corkstone did not trust Riley and kept an extra-close eye on her at all times, and often did not even let her leave class to use the bathroom.

- One of Riley's adopted grandparents in her Senior Friends program was convicted of second-degree murder–at age ninety-three.

THIRTY
Off

The morning after I visited Alex at his house, I have a doctor's appointment. It's just a checkup—nothing to worry about, of course—but since cell phones aren't allowed to be on in the doctor's office, and I'm not exactly the type of girl who needs social media 24-7, I don't bother to check it when I leave the doctor's office.

Or when I stop at Starbucks.

So it isn't until I pull into the parking lot that I notice something is different. *Off.* About fifteen students are clustered outside the glass door that leads to the gym corridor, and they are just *standing* there. Talking. Leaning in. And no one—not a student aide, or a teacher, or anyone, is telling them to get to class.

AMANDA K. MORGAN

I check my phone. It is definitely class time. It isn't a passing period or anything.

And there are *thirteen* texts I've missed. I type in my passcode to open them.

Mom (1)

Kolbie (7)

Neta (5)

Mom: Can you stop at the grocery store before you come home tonight and pick up onion powder please? Hope your appointment went well. XOXO.

Kolbie: OMG DID YOU GUYS HEAR

Neta: YES. What is going on?!?!?!?!

Kolbie: I have NO IDEA

Kolbie: JUST GONE JUST LIKE THAT

Neta: Everyone is freaking out

Kolbie: Mrs. Tanner isn't even bothering to teach the lesson right now.

Neta: Is she crying, because there are girls in my class actually crying.

Kolbie: Yep cryers here too. It can't be that serious can it? I'm sure it's just a misunderstanding. Likeeee probably dentist appointment for wisdom teeth or something

Neta: yeah well I heard they called the police so . . .

Kolbie: OH SHIT WHAT

Neta: Yep. It's not like him, though. I would freak if I were his wife.

Kolbie: It's getting real. This is SCARY

I click out of my texts and slip my phone into my purse. I could ask Kolbie and Neta what is going on, but if they're in class, they won't be able to respond immediately. Plus, based on the cur-

220

SUCH A GOOD GIRL

rent tone of their messages, they're likely to be more than a little dramatic.

So I stop by the students gathered of the steps leading into the corridor. "What's going on?" I ask.

A freshman girl with pretty braids detaches herself from the group, eager to share gossip with me. She looks both ways, like she's afraid someone might see her. "Mr. Belrose didn't show up for his classes this morning."

And then, everything inside of me falls apart systemically.

First, my heart seems to stop. Then my stomach curls.

And then my legs feel like they detach and my bones vanish.

"What?" I ask, very faintly. I want to rest my hand on her shoulder, to get my bearings.

"He just didn't show up," she repeats. "And no one can get ahold of him or find him or anything." She bounces a little bit, like this is very exciting news. "People are really worried. There are people praying in the library and other people trying to break it up because this is, like, a public school."

I think I say something back, but I'm not sure.

I fumble my way toward the locker room, which happens to have the closest bathrooms, and am promptly sick into the toilet, which is where Neta finds me twenty minutes later, still puking my guts out.

"Are you okay?" she asks.

I nod, wiping my mouth off with a clump of thin toilet paper that clings to my chin. "I think it was just something the doctor did."

221

She feels my forehead. "You're not that warm. Still, you should probably go to the nurse's office. I'll walk you down there."

I shake my head. I need to stay here. I need to figure out what is going on. If I'm home in bed, I'll have to rely on text messages, and I can't even be overeager about those or it'll look really suspicious. I wash my mouth out and grab a stick of mint gum from my backpack. "I'm okay," I insist. I try to pull my hair around my face a little bit, so I don't look so sticky and pale. I am not one of those crying girls in the hallway. I am not Thea, who is clawing at the wall, acting like her world has ended.

I am fine. Getting overly excited about a teacher failing to show for class would be decidedly not Riley behavior.

"Did you hear about Belrose?" Neta asks, her voice low. "Weird, right?"

I nod. "Really weird. Have you heard anything?"

"He didn't show for a makeup test for Gabriella Hernandez this morning, but she just went to the office and reported it so they could mark that she hadn't ditched, you know? And they didn't think much of it. But then he didn't show for his first-period class. *Or* his second period. And he's still not here."

I swallow hard around my gum. My mouth still holds to the sick-sweet-sour taste of vomit, and my stomach feels like there is something living inside of it, thrashing and angry and vile and scratching at the lining, trying to get out.

Did he try to leave Jacqueline and she—did something?

Or did Jacqueline find out about me?

Or maybe . . . maybe he just slept in.

SUCH A GOOD GIRL

Maybe that's all.

It happens. People get tired. And Alex has been under a *lot* of stress lately. While we're walking, I pull out my phone and send him a quick e-mail.

Are you okay?

But I'm not the only one worried. The school is a mess. Students are in the hallways, along with teachers. But it's not loud. No one is yelling or running. Everyone is just staring around like they're looking for something and speaking to each other in hushed tones.

The minutes slip by strangely, like time is folding in on itself, too fast and too slow all at once.

And still no Alex Belrose.

"Let's walk by the office," Neta suggests. "I'm not in the mood for fifth period."

I nod. I'm not, either. I know I'm supposed to be toeing the line on account of my nonexistent French grade problem, but I don't really care.

Kolbie catches up with us in the hallway, and we walk to the office together, and that's when we see *her*.

"Holy shit," Kolbie says.

"What?" Neta asks.

"That's his wife," I murmur.

And there she is, in high-heeled boots and a big black hat, like she just stepped off a runway, just inside the glass enclosure of the main office. She looks like a pretty caged butterfly, flapping meaninglessly inside an enclosure. She's an homage to

223

the reality star: all image and no substance, ready to be photographed, calm and put-together just in case there's some dramatic tragedy. What the hell would she be doing *here*? Shouldn't she be at the police station, if she's worried? I stare at her. How convenient that she's in all black. Already in mourning for her missing husband. She couldn't even wait a day to soak up the attention and pity.

"Does this mean she doesn't know where he is either?" Neta asks.

"I would guess so," Kolbie says. "A wife doesn't really have to be here to call you in sick, does she?"

I don't say what I already know: she's supposed to be in Vegas. Or at least she was, until last night.

I frown. Why *is* she back? Did she fly back when she heard her husband didn't show up to work?

Is she looking for him here? Did they call her in? Or is she just here to throw her own little pity party?

Jacqueline turns toward us, and Kolbie and Neta gasp, but I don't move. I lock eyes with her.

She pauses, her long eyelashes fluttering.

She doesn't even look upset. She looks normal, like maybe she's just dropping off something for him. There is no trace of concern anywhere on her radiant face.

And then she walks out of the office, like nothing happened, her heels echoing on the dirty tile. She stalks out the door and down the sidewalk, where her teal car is parked illegally in the loading zone.

SUCH A GOOD GIRL

But that's how I know.

She knows more than she's letting on.

And maybe that has something to do with me. Maybe she knows about Alex and me. Or maybe Alex had to run away to finally be free of her.

THIRTY-ONE
Nothing

He hasn't responded. Forty-eight hours and Alex Belrose has not responded.

I stare at my phone as I walk. It's not like this is new. It's not like he just supplies me with attention whenever I want it. I'm obviously not that important to him anyway.

I want to e-mail him again. But e-mailing someone who is potentially missing is probably not a great idea. I don't want them tracing anything back to me. I don't want them finding a hair on his couch and connecting the DNA or something.

I stick my phone in my purse and keep to my route: the Belrose house. And not my normal route. It's a long walk, but I don't care. I'm not parking a car anywhere close. I wore an old jacket from

SUCH A GOOD GIRL

the back of my closet and tugged on mittens, two wool scarves, and a thick knit hat, and I even grabbed two hand warmers from my dad's hunting gear to keep in my pockets if it gets really cold. I haven't had to use them—I've been walking so much that I'm not particularly chilled beyond my cheeks, which are stinging a bit.

Normally, I'd be at cheer tonight, but with the hubbub, all after-school activities were canceled. Everyone's on edge. Everyone's a little scared. Any laughter in the school sounds strange and alien. And they've brought in Mr. Anderburg, a young, twitchy man, as the substitute French teacher . . . and he doesn't understand two words of the language, I'm pretty sure. He sort of stands at the front of the class in baggy clothes, stuttery and out of place, and the whole room feels pale and odd and scared without Belrose at the helm.

Everyone whispers. All the time.

I walk faster. I'm almost there. I think of the steps I am taking and my fitness wristband, but I don't want anything tracking me here. My location tracker on my smartphone has been off basically since I got it. I hate people knowing where I am at all times. It's creepy.

I like my steps untraceable.

I stop deliberately short of the Belrose house, and it looks just like it always has, like Alex is just waiting for me to slip in through the back gate and into the den, where he'll be waiting with French poetry and a kiss. Only he isn't. Only I've checked my e-mail ten thousand times and he's nowhere, and no one knows anything, especially not me, and it hurts somewhere strange and deep in me where I didn't know it was possible to hurt.

227

I study the house from as close as I dare, but I can't see anything of note. Just the same old house, looking the same old way, and nothing to show that anyone is missing or that anything has happened at all.

I feel strange and let down. Somehow I felt like maybe if I were in the neighborhood, he'd want to come back. He'd sense I was here and pop up, and be happy to see me.

If he could.

But there's nothing. Just the sound of the fir trees moving and distant wind chimes.

I swallow hard, resisting the urge to push through the gate and try the back door. I turn away instead, and walk through the trees, trudging back in the direction of my house.

When I get home, though, I force myself to concentrate. I sit at the desk in my room and finish my homework. I double-check all my answers even though I know I'm right. I double-check them even though I'm certain my teachers don't care right now either.

Everyone's mind is elsewhere.

Nothing like this has ever happened before.

Neta texts me.

COME OVER. I'M BOREDDDDDDDDDDDDD.

I'm not. But I need something else to think about besides Alex. Something else to do besides check my e-mail and pace the floor of my room, wearing a path in my rug.

"You came!" she squeals at me when I walk through the door, and hugs me. She looks good. A lot better since the funeral, actually, although I suppose that's not hard, since the funeral was

SUCH A GOOD GIRL

pretty much the lowest I'd ever seen her. For a few days after the service she stopped wearing makeup because she kept crying it off so quickly, but she has it back on today and she's actually sort of smiling.

"You okay?" I ask cautiously.

"Just glad you're here," she says, but if I look hard I can see a little bit of sadness underneath her excitement. "Come downstairs. I have TLC on and I made brownies."

Neta is basically Martha Stewart (minus the jail time) in the kitchen, and I cannot resist her brownies. She also knows I'm not the type of girl to eat one bite of brownie and feel bad about it for a million years. I'll eat, like, twelve and feel pretty great about it, honestly. And then I might get a stomachache and decide it was a bad idea later, but I prefer to live in the moment. And in this moment, I need brownies in my life.

I am a girl who knows what she wants, after all.

"Do you have ice cream?"

"Rocky road."

"You're the light of my life, Neta Adriana Castillo."

She flips her hair. "I know."

We run downstairs like we're middle schoolers again. TLC is playing reruns of *Say Yes to the Dress*, which we both know is staged, but we don't care. The entire pan of brownies (minus two squares) are sitting, precut, on the floor in front of the television. Neta disappears for a moment and brings back two pints of store-brand ice cream—one fudge chocolate, one mint chocolate chip.

"Sorry, no rocky road," she says apologetically, dropping a

spoon in my lap, and we grab a bunch of old blankets and pillows and sit on top of them.

"Thanks for coming over," she says. "I needed some distractions."

"So did I," I say. "This whole thing at school with Mr. Belrose is nuts, right?"

She nods. "I heard, like, he got *kidnapped*." She pulls a blanket around her shoulders.

"What? From who?" I sit up a little straighter.

"Lilah Gilbert, actually. She said that he was taken by someone who was pissed about a grade. Isn't that insane?"

I sink back down into the pile of blankets. Nothing Lilah Gilbert says is likely to be anywhere close to the truth. In fourth grade, she pulled two hundred dollars out of a Cracker Jack box, claiming it was a prize, but she actually stole it from Mr. Jeppard's wallet, which he figured out during a spelling test when his wife came by to pick up the cash she was supposed to buy a used crib with. Of course, Elijah Piper pointed right at Lilah and mentioned her lucky Cracker Jack winnings, and Mr. Jeppard was so mad, he didn't stop at sending Lilah to the office. The cops actually arrested her for theft. She got suspended for two weeks, and when she returned, she was transferred next door to Mrs. Dones's class, which we were all pretty jealous about because Mrs. Dones let everyone call her Angelica and play music during reading hour.

"What do you think happened?" Neta asks. She's mashing brownie into her mint chocolate chip ice cream.

For a second, I want to tell her everything. I want to tell her

SUCH A GOOD GIRL

about our nights together, and how Alex kisses, all of the meals he has cooked for me, and the French poetry, and the promises to leave Jacqueline, and how we were really going to be together. I want to tell her how he betrayed me and how somehow even though I sort of hate him a little, I think I actually love him.

But that's all ridiculous, of course.

So the moment passes. I grab a spoonful of her mint-and-brownie mess. "His wife is a little nutty, isn't she?" I ask. "Maybe they should start there."

Neta grabs the remote and starts paging through the guide, bored with the white-wedding-dressed women on the screen. "Maybe. Hey, did I tell you I'm talking to someone new?"

I blink at her. "No, you didn't!" I don't point out that I've been a pretty poor friend because I've very nearly been doing my teacher.

"His name is Chase, and he's friends with Jamal too, I guess. After the whole Sandeep fiasco, I suppose Kolbie thought I deserved a shot—so Chase just happened to be in town just after visiting his aunt and uncle or something. So we went to a movie with Kolbie and Jamal, and then, I don't know, I think we're a thing or something."

"You think you're a thing?" I ask, trying to emulate her level of excitement while my heart is dropping. "Have you talked about it?"

"Kind of. I mean, he's going back this weekend, and we're supposed to hang out. He's taking me to a nice dinner, and we've texted every night. See? We're texting right now." She thrusts her iPhone at me, showing three (3) new texts from Chase Abrams.

"You really like him." A little of the strange jealousy that rose when I realized that Kolbie and Neta have a life without me fades. Neta really needs a distraction right now. And if that's Chase . . . well, then, that's good for her. And I'm glad. She needs something positive in her life.

She wiggles a little. "Yeah, kind of. I just wish he were here, you know? So we could hang out as often as RJ and I did. RJ was always just—around when I needed him."

"Yeah. I get that."

I wish Alex were here too. Everything feels strange now. Before Alex, I would have been fine sitting here in the basement with Neta, eating ice cream and talking about guys and watching reality shows.

And now it doesn't feel like enough.

The doorbell rings upstairs. "Expecting someone?" I ask, but Neta shakes her head and chooses reruns of *Teen Mom* . . . but then Rob Samuels comes stomping down the stairs. One of his sneakers is untied and he's grinning and holding a liter of Dr Pepper and a big brown paper bag that says *SMILEY'S*, the name of the local grocery store. A big tear runs up the side.

"Hey!" he says. "What's up?"

I want to drag Neta in the bathroom and force her to explain herself, but she just points to the recliner near her shoulder. "What's up, Rob?" she asks. "Grab a seat."

He sits down. I shoot her a look. She could have at least told me he was coming. I feel slightly intruded upon. I thought it was girls' night.

"I heard it was junk food time," he says, and tears open the

SUCH A GOOD GIRL

brown bag and leans forward to dump it out between us on the blankets. An array of candy flows out in a sugar waterfall: caramels, little packets of Sour Patch Kids and Swedish Fish, chocolate truffles, red and pink Starburst, and even fun-size packages of Skittles.

I relent a little.

"I'll get a little ice for the soda," he offers. "Are you done with the ice cream? I can put it back in the freezer if you want." He collects the ice cream containers and runs up the stairs, like he knows exactly where everything is.

"What?" Neta asks innocently. "He's *helpful.*"

I glower. "Helpful, huh?"

"This has nothing to do with you. I swear to God. He's just been sweet to me at school. That's all. So I told him he could hang out with us, and obviously he is cool because he is basically a girl, snack-wise. I mean, look at this. His sweets game is on point. There is not a Funyun or beef jerky in the mix."

She throws herself back on the pile of candy, doing a snow angel in the mess. I giggle in spite of myself.

"I guess. But I love Funyuns. And beef jerky."

Neta makes a face.

Rob stomps back down the stairs, three glasses filled with ice balanced in his hands. "Ladies first," he says without any trace of irony, and fills our glasses with cold Dr Pepper.

I observe him. He does seem sort of harmless, and if Neta's the one who wants him here, I don't exactly care. He sinks back into the chair and grabs a chocolate truffle off the floor.

233

AMANDA K. MORGAN

"You can't tell my friends I'm here," he tells me, popping the truffle into his mouth. "I'd lose major points. Oh, hey, is this *Teen Mom*? I don't think I've seen this one." He leans forward and scoops up a couple of Starburst.

I watch him for a few seconds longer, but he sort of seems content just staring at the TV, so I nudge Neta.

"So, Chase this weekend, huh?" I ask, and she practically bubbles over with excitement. I let her talk over the television, which normally drives me crazy. Somebody needs a little happy in their lives, and if it can't be me, it might as well be Neta.

THIRTY-TWO
Fake

"Nothing."

My brother shakes his head. "This is bad. I just have this feeling, you know? It's in my gut. It feels like *shit*." He puts his hand on his stomach.

"Yeah," I say. I'm sprawled out across the couch in the living room, an old *People* magazine open under my arm, and Ethan is rocking back and forth in the recliner. It makes a small squeak every time he moves.

He won't shut up about Alex.

I give up on the magazine and pretend like I'm watching some stupid cartoon, only I don't know anything that's going on and I think I might be sick at any second. It rises up from the top of my stomach and sits at the base of my throat.

"There are search parties out, and they're just not successful. They're in all the parks and stuff, but they're not finding anything. I mean, *anything*. And the cops have questioned his wife, and I don't think she's a 'person of interest' or whatever. And maybe it's good that they haven't found him, but you know what everyone's saying, right?"

I don't want him to answer. I can't hear the answer. I don't want him to say it.

"They're saying that he's *dead*." He pauses, staring at the characters leapfrogging across the television. "Can you believe it? Someone I went to high school with? Just dead, just like that? Life is screwed up. I mean, I never knew anyone that *died* before."

He says it like it's final and done and inarguable and just a thing.

"I'm sure he's not dead," I say, but even as I say them, the words are tinny and false in my ears. I stand up, wishing I were numb, and walk to the little half bath by the kitchen, where I am very quietly ill before wiping my mouth and returning to the TV. I sink into the couch, my skin clammy, and pull a throw over my legs.

"I keep calling him, you know?" Ethan says. "I bet I called him twenty times. All of us have. It's like I expect him to answer, but he never does." He pauses, jiggling the remote. "Have you heard anything?"

"Nothing," I say, and my throat clams up a little. Are they going to start combing his house for DNA? Then what? Are they going to

SUCH A GOOD GIRL

find me? Would it even matter? I'm sure I'm not in a database or anything, on account of never having committed any real crimes.

It's not like anyone would suspect me—anyone. No one knows I've ever been there. No neighbors have ever seen me enter or exit.

I don't think.

My blood feels oddly thick in my veins, and I run to the little half bath again, but there is nothing left in my stomach.

The next day at school, the mood is tense, and I can hardly get through my classes. The teachers feel pretty much the same way, and they barely give us any homework—which is a good and bad thing, because it means my mind has room to wander, and the only thing anyone can really think about is Belrose. Unless you're Neta, and then you're thinking about Chase.

Or Rob Samuels, blond-headed wonder boy, and in that case you're thinking about me.

"Hey, Stone!" He jogs up to me after school, as I'm headed out toward the parking lot. He grins at me, really big, in a way that nobody has really been grinning in the past week at all, and it's rather like shouting in a church.

In the middle of a funeral.

I cringe at the thought.

"Hey, Rob."

He falls into step beside me. "So, um, I had fun the other night chilling with you guys."

"Um, that's cool. Me too."

"Is it okay if I walk you to your car?" he asks as he walks me

237

to my car, past everyone else still walking with their heads down, voices muted.

I frown. "That's fine." I stop at my car, feeling awkward. "Um, thanks, Rob. I appreciate it."

He still has that big, shouty grin on. "Sure."

"Um, thanks." I make to get in the car, but Rob sort of looks around and moves his feet over the ground, but doesn't leave.

"Riley," he says, "are you okay?"

I frown at him. "Why do you ask that?"

He kicks at the gravel in the street and leans up against my door, but he doesn't meet my eyes. "You've just seemed different lately. And not different like everyone else is being different, just, like, lately. But *different* different. Not to seem creepy or anything, but I notice you. I pay attention to you. You're a smart person, and you're a good person to take note of, but I can tell something is wrong, Riley. And I just wanted to see if I could, you know, help in some kind of way." His cheeks flush a little.

I bite the inside of my cheek to keep from tearing up. Someone noticed. Rob Samuels, out of everyone, actually *noticed*.

I hug him, right there, in front of all the students still walking out of the school into the parking lot. Let them think whatever they want.

I needed that.

"Why do you care?" I ask. My words sound mean, even to my ears, but I don't intend it that way. I really want to know. It's not like I've treated him all that well. It's not like I deserve it.

"I just do."

SUCH A GOOD GIRL

I look at him, just standing there, and his smile has lessened a little bit, so it's just . . . nice. Maybe I should have a boyfriend. It couldn't hurt. Especially not now. Maybe it would even keep . . . people . . . from looking at me suspiciously.

"Do you want to come over and hang out?"

The question is out before I fully consider it, and Rob looks at me, his eyes big and shiny and the loud smile back. "Yes."

I let him follow me to my house in his car and make him park at the curb instead of in the driveway, and when he follows me in I take him down to the basement, where we have a big-screen TV and an old L-shape couch that's perfect for long movies and cold days.

"I didn't bring any snacks," he says, and he looks miserable, like he has let me down in some unforgivable way.

"It's okay," I tell him. "I'll go get something from the kitchen."

My parents aren't home. I'm hoping if they see his car when they get off work they'll just think it's one of the neighbors being annoying or something. They hate it when someone parks close. I'm not ready to explain Rob to them just yet anyway. I run upstairs and grab a bag of my mom's Lite Butter Skinny-Woman Popcorn before tossing it into the microwave.

I watch it turn. The microwave hums and rattles where the plate isn't set quite right.

What am I doing?

Why am I doing this?

The bag slowly starts to inflate, the kernels cracking and popping. I make myself turn away. I am a hostess, aren't I? So why don't

239

I care right now? Why aren't I excited that there's a guy downstairs who really, really cares about me?

I grab two cans of Coke from the fridge and pull a couple of paper towels from the roll before grabbing the popcorn out of the microwave and walking it back downstairs. Rob has moved from the couch to the television, where he's checking out my parents' DVD collection.

"*Die Hard 2* and *The Notebook*?" he asks. "This is a tough choice. What do you want to watch?"

I lift a shoulder and open the bag of popcorn, my fingers burning a little from the steam that escapes from the top. I set it down and blow on them.

Rob stands and catches my hand in his.

"Let me," he says.

He raises my fingers to his lips and blows, very gently, but the air from his lips is warm. His fingers are rough on my palm.

It doesn't feel right.

Nothing feels right.

I pull away without meaning to.

"I'll just run them under cold water for a second, okay? Choose a good movie. Um, maybe an action movie."

I don't wait for his reaction. I run off to the bathroom and shut the door behind me. Maybe this was a bad idea. He wants me, and I know he wants me, and I'm just using him again. I have to hold him far away, because I can't make myself be with him.

I shove my fingers under the cold water even though they don't hurt anymore and count to twenty. And then I dry off my hands and walk back into the little den.

SUCH A GOOD GIRL

Where the opening credits for *Pride and Prejudice* are playing on the TV.

"I thought you'd like it," Rob says, looking a little guilty.

I sigh and sit on the opposite end of the couch. "It's fine."

He scoots a cushion closer, and I stick my feet out so he can't sit next to me.

"Do you want popcorn?" he asks.

I stand up and grab a handful from the bag and a can of Coke, then return to my seat. "I love this movie."

"Me too," he says.

But for someone who loves *Pride and Prejudice,* he spends more time watching me than Keira Knightley.

THIRTY-THREE
Struggle

"So tell us more about this Rob boy," Mom says. "He seemed so sweet! I don't know why you haven't brought him around before, honestly."

Of course Mom loved him. And I wouldn't have even had to introduce Rob last night if he hadn't stayed after the movie to clean, insisting that we'd left crumbs on the floor from the popcorn.

"Kernels are so hard to get out of carpet," he'd said, and then actually started opening closets and stuff until he found my Mom's fancy new Hoover she ordered off the Home Shopping Network, and even though I'd told him "please, no," he started vacuuming the floor and folding up throw blankets and putting the DVD into its case and doing stuff he most definitely did not need to do.

SUCH A GOOD GIRL

So of course my mom came downstairs to see what the hell her daughter was doing vacuuming so late at night (or at all), and saw Rob, who of course ma'am-ed his way into my mom's heart immediately, and I'm relatively certain she had him mapped out as my prom date and possibly as my husband before he'd left.

Rob does that to mothers.

I remember in fifth grade, he'd always be first to volunteer to help the class mothers hand out birthday cupcakes. Back then, he was stocky and cute and his blond hair was always getting in his eyes, and no matter whose birthday it was, he would always save me the cupcake with the most frosting.

Of course, now he's the kind of guy who would be cast in an after-school special. If I want to avoid being engaged by the end of the year, I'm going to have to figure something out.

Today is Saturday and the heat is broken. Apparently, while doing a major renovation on the house at the end of the street, the construction workers accidentally messed up the gas line, and now the entire neighborhood is waiting for the gas company to get it fixed. As a result, my mother got this idea that we should all have breakfast in the living room together under blankets and be a *family*. So she talked my father into making waffles and bacon and eggs and called Ethan and now we're sort of comfortable, weighted down under huge piles of old throws that smell just a bit dusty, with heating pads plugged in underneath. The sky outside is a deceptive blue, too light for the odd weather.

Even Esther is here, sharing a recliner with my brother, the swell of her stomach hidden under the pile of blankets. They have

243

one plate of food between them, and her head is on his shoulder and he's smiling.

The TV is on, quietly, and for just a little bit, I feel happy, with me and my family and Esther, while we talk quietly and eat our waffles with extra butter and syrup and I realize I can't remember the last time I felt this content with them.

"Your mother says you had someone over last night," Dad says.

"He was very nice." Mom glows. "His name was Robert Samuels. He's a good boy."

Good boy. Good girl.

How *fitting*.

My dad opens his mouth to say something else, but Ethan interrupts, leaning forward and nearly spilling Esther out of his lap. He wraps his arms around her, and she grabs on to the plate, but the fork falls onto the rug.

"Turn that up, okay?"

The TV shows a picture of a pretty blond reporter holding a stack of papers. A picture of Alex, taken at the last school photo day, his HARTSVILLE HIGH tag clipped to his shirt, is shown in the upper right-hand corner. His smile is practiced and smooth, and his face is neatly shaven.

". . . possible signs of a struggle at the Belrose residence. Mrs. Belrose was taken into custody for questioning, but has been released. The police chief is asking that anyone with any information about this case please come forward immediately."

My heart feels like paper that has been lit on fire and is blackening and curling up from the edges.

SUCH A GOOD GIRL

It's a strangely familiar feeling.

She killed him. I *know* she killed him. But it's not like I can just go down to the police station and be like, "Hey, I just happen to know my sort-of boyfriend teacher probably got slaughtered by his wife."

Was it my fault she did it? Or did Alex actually grow the balls to ask her for a divorce and maybe she just flipped out?

Am I going to be brought in next?

"What about your grades?" my dad asks. "Now that he's out, who's going to fix them?"

Mom puts her hands on her chest. "You're right. I didn't even think of that. Should we call the school? This is bad, Riley, isn't it? He was going to help you."

Of course. Alex is missing and my parents are worried about my grades. They're not worried about him possibly being dead or the fact that he was most likely murdered by his crazy wife.

"Um, I did extra credit. So it'll be fine."

I don't mention that the bad grades were all bullshit anyway, and that I checked the grade book because the substitute is completely lame and bought my story when I said I needed to check that Belrose had recorded a grade for the essay I'd turned in before he'd disappeared.

He'd never actually recorded a single bad grade. Not one.

But I'd known that anyway. Of course.

"This is so fucked up," Ethan mutters. "What has it been now? A week and a half? And *nothing*?"

Esther pushes his hair back. "Were you guys in touch?"

245

AMANDA K. MORGAN

Ethan mumbles something. Because they weren't. He is just one of those people, hanging on to an old connection, wishing he'd called or texted or something before his friend went missing.

And then everything is weird and quiet and I can hear my dad chewing his bacon, which he likes black and burnt.

"Rob is great," I say into the quiet. "He's really cool."

"Are you going to see him again?" my mother asks.

I nod. "Yep. Definitely." I take a sip of the coffee my mother made as her contribution. It's not very strong and could use sugar and creamer. Suddenly I'm hot. Too hot for all the blankets and the plate in my lap and waffles and coffee. I push them off and head for the kitchen.

"Where are you going, honey?" Mom asks, like I'm going out into a blizzard and not just a cold house.

"I need sugar."

Instead of going back to the living room, I stand in the kitchen. The floor is icy.

The cops obviously aren't taking Jacqueline seriously. And maybe that means I will have to.

And if Jacqueline isn't above killing, maybe I'm not either. And that goes double if Alex told Jacqueline anything about me.

Oh my God.

What if Alex told Jacqueline something about me?

I'm stirring sugar into my coffee, hopping back and forth on the cold tile floor, when the doorbell rings.

"I'll get it," I yell into the living room. The rest of my family is still likely cocooned into their blankets, so I run to the door,

246

SUCH A GOOD GIRL

wishing I'd made it back to my bedroom for socks. I wiggle my toes into the softness of the rug and swing the door open, hoping it's the repairman, telling us our heat will be kicking back on shortly.

It's not.

It's Neta and Rob.

Neta bursts in without even saying hello. "Did you just see the news?" she asks. She lowers her voice. "We had to come over. Like . . . holy shit."

I wrap my arms around myself. "You chose the wrong house. Heat is out."

Rob smiles at me. "We don't care."

Neta fake-grins. "Yeah, we don't care." She imitates Rob and gives me this huge fake wink.

I lead them downstairs, away from the family meeting in the living room, and pull the remaining musty blankets out of the closet under the stairs. I find an old space heater and plug it in, and when I turn back Neta is on one end of the couch and Rob is on the other.

So I sit in the middle.

And cover up with the thinnest blanket.

"Do you want to share?" Rob scoots a little closer.

"I'm good."

The space heater starts to make an odd metallic noise. I hope it's not going to explode. My mom is always going on about space heaters exploding and starting stuff on fire and everyone dying.

247

"So do you think he's dead?" Neta asks. And she looks sad, actually. She wraps her arms around herself. "I just—I can't. I can't deal. But if there are signs of an actual struggle—"

"Then why are they just now finding them?" I interrupt. "This is all too weird. Why is this all just now happening?"

"Sometimes the cops don't release stuff right away." Rob pulls the blanket around his shoulders, and I turn on the television to a pop music channel to cover the sound of our voices. I don't want my parents to try to eavesdrop on our conversation, and since they're suddenly interested in Rob, they might actually try.

Weird that it took a guy for them to notice that their daughter was here, around, a sentient being instead of a picture to straighten on a wall. Weird that I wasn't enough on my own when I was being the perfect child and pinning awards and ribbons to my dream board and filling my bank account I can't touch with grants and my future with scholarships. It took a boy and bad grades to even get them to look at me.

Weird that being accepted to the right colleges wasn't enough. Weird that all my friends want to do is talk about men and what it takes to get them to look at you and what happens when they touch you and all the things you might have done wrong when they don't.

At the end of the day, that's really all that's important. And who are we without male approval?

And look what I have with Rob on my arm.

Approval.

Attention.

Weird.

SUCH A GOOD GIRL

Ethan was right.

"Why don't they release anything?" Neta asks. "I mean, that doesn't make sense. Nothing makes sense about this. Why would anyone kill Mr. Belrose? He was *perfect*."

"If they put everything out there and someone comes forward with information they haven't put out, well, then they know that person is involved with the crime somehow, you know?"

It makes sense.

Which means I can't say anything about Jacqueline.

Anything.

"Maybe there wasn't even a crime," I say. "What makes you so sure there was a crime? Maybe it was an accident. Maybe he just got stressed out. Maybe he just left his wife."

"I'm sure the police are investigating all of that. But they have to face the facts." Rob's hand appears from under his blanket and rests on my leg, and moves back and forth. "They haven't found a trace of him. And usually that means—something really bad is going on. The longer he's missing, the more likely it is he's dead."

I swallow hard. I want to move away. I want to push him away. I want to be anywhere but here. The blanket is thin enough that I can feel the pressure of each of his fingers. My skin feels strange and dirty.

"But it's Mr. Belrose," Neta says. "He's just—it's just—he can't be."

I stare at Rob's hand.

"He can't be," I repeat. "He's probably just lost or something."

Rob's hand moves.

I hate him.

249

I'm using him. I hate myself. And I'm using him. I need to end this, and I need to end this now, and I need to stop gossiping about whether Alex is dead, and I need to get him away from me and get him to quit touching me.

I am going to scream.

Neta draws her legs up on the couch. "How do you know so much about everything, Rob?"

"*Law and Order* addict. I'm an expert about this kind of stuff."

I stand up, and Rob's hand slides off my leg. "Do you guys want anything from the kitchen? Drinks? Coffee?"

"I can get it," Rob says, hopping up. "Do you want a Coke, Riley?"

"Something hot. A cappuccino, maybe," I suggest, knowing the machine isn't hooked up and it'll take him at least ten minutes to get it going.

"Me too," Neta says.

Rob runs up the stairs toward the kitchen and Neta focuses on me.

"You can't get rid of him," she says, reading my mind. "He's basically perfect. And you need a good guy, right?"

I stare at her. Of course. Women *need* men.

A good guy.

"Sure, Neta."

Weird.

THIRTY-FOUR
Brownies

Honestly, I didn't expect to learn a lot from the Senior Friends program I orchestrated, where I paired up students and cool senior citizens, but I have to say, Ms. Glenda did pass on the perfect brownie recipe. I happen to know her goddaughter, Dana, *really* had her heart set on the secret family recipe, but Glenda said that Dana had a real mean streak and she'd rather give it to someone who would appreciate it, and who am I to ignore the wishes of a dying old woman? Plus, Glenda said one day I'd need to make a decent pan of brownies, and I suppose she was right. I also suppose I didn't expect to make them for my ex-boyfriend's potential widow.

Baking is, after all, what you do when someone is grieving. Last time I went to my neighbor's house after her husband had died, everyone showed up with more pies and casseroles than she could have ever eaten. My parents showed up with a Jell-O salad with whipped cream and crushed pretzels on top.

I stir the batter, wash and put away the dishes, and have the brownies out of the oven before my parents can get home to ask what I'm up to. And then I head to the unhappiest house I can possibly think of.

A very familiar house.

The Belrose house.

I go with my brownies and my most perfect A-plus-student smile and a plan.

And I go because I can't stand it anymore even though there are a thousand reasons why I shouldn't.

I wear a perfect green sweater with a pocket on the right side of my chest, an A-line skirt that falls at just below my knees, and my National Honor Society pin. My hair is smoothed back into a careful ponytail, around which I have tied a dark pink ribbon that I've fastened into a neat bow so that two ends hang perfectly down on either side of my head. I in no way look like a harlot when I ring the doorbell with my plate of brownies. I know Jacqueline is home, because her obnoxiously bright car is parked at the end of the sidewalk.

For a moment, I don't hear anything, and then there are quiet little footsteps. The front door swings open, and then there's Jacqueline, adorned in a thin black dress, her makeup done with absolute perfection. A black fedora is perched on the top of her head and she has donned tiny little fingerless gloves. It's as if she's waiting to be photographed as the sad, sexy widow.

SUCH A GOOD GIRL

Like this has all been planned.

"I don't want Girl Scout cookies." Her voice is clipped, and she begins to close the door.

"I'm actually here on behalf of Mr. Belrose's French honors students," I say, my voice high and chirpy. "We just wanted to drop in on you to see how you were doing and give you these." I hold out the foil-covered pan.

"What are they?" she asks, turning her nose up a bit like maybe I'm trying to poison her.

Which wouldn't be a bad idea.

"Homemade brownies. From scratch. We're just so worried about you, Mrs. Belrose. We can't imagine what you're going through right now."

She gives me a long look, then cracks open her door, just a bit wider. "Well, okay then. Come on in."

I bite back a smile.

Excellent.

If the cops find my DNA in the Belrose house and someone traces it back to me, I want to say I've been in the house for a reason, even if it's giving brownies to a falsely grieving widow who doesn't look like she's been crying at all.

And if I happen to do a little detective work in the meantime . . . well. That's fine.

I sit down on the couch first, balancing my tray in my lap. "Maybe I should put these in the kitchen. They're still warm. Um, where is it?"

Because of course I haven't been here before.

253

"Just through there," she says, pointing to the doorway toward the cheery little kitchen. "Leave them on the table."

I do as I'm told.

"Those don't have any peanuts or anything in them, do they? I'm just terribly allergic. I mean, I would totally *die* if you gave me peanuts," Jacqueline says. Her hand raises her to throat. She speaks with an odd accent—maybe with the slightest French lilt, which is obnoxious, since I'm pretty sure she's originally from a small town in Texas.

"No," I say. Regrettably. I file away the knowledge. So Jacqueline has a severe food allergy. I could use that.

I sit back on the couch and cross my legs.

"How are you, Mrs. Belrose?" I furrow my brow, showing concern. I am a puppet.

So is she.

She wipes away a tear that isn't there.

"It's been so hard—uh—what did your say your name was?"

"Riley Stone."

I study her face. There is no flicker of recognition. Her eyebrows don't raise.

So he didn't tell her anything. If he said he was going to leave her, I wasn't a reason why.

"I'm going to be the valedictorian," I explain. "I am very good at French."

"Good for you, honey," she says. She reaches forward and pats me very lightly on the wrist, her palm flat and stiff. Is she always this weird?

SUCH A GOOD GIRL

For a moment, we're just silent, and I look out the picture window, trying not to think about all the other times I've looked out that very same picture window, and who was sitting next to me, and how much better I felt before.

"Is there anything—have you heard or found anything?" I ask. "We're just all so worried—I had to ask."

She smiles at me, but her teeth are hidden behind her lips. "There is a reason why I wear black, my darling."

"What?"

Her eyes flutter, like she's holding back tears that aren't really there. "A wife knows in her heart when she is widowed. And make no mistake. My husband is dead. I don't know how and I don't know why, but the other half of my heart has stopped beating. I feel it here." She presses her thin hand to her chest. "He is gone."

"How can you be sure?"

She looks at me sharply. "You would know if you ever really loved someone, Rayna," she says, forgetting my name already. "He is dead and has left me and all I can do is get used to it, and it's time for everyone else to do the same, and stop calling this a rescue mission. My love is dead. He's *dead*."

I stare at her. She's nuts. She's as much as confessing here. Why say someone is dead with so much certainty if you didn't kill him?

Why aren't the cops holding her?

"But how do you know?"

"I have premonitions about these things, my dear. It does no good to ask questions." She leans toward me. "Thank you for the snacks, sweet girl, but I think it's time for you to leave."

255

Right. Premonitions. How very intuitive of her. And that's a reason to give up on your husband if you didn't absolutely murder him in cold blood.

I stand. "Um, well let me know if you need anything else, okay?"

She takes my hand, and her skin is papery and cold and reminds me of an old woman. "Thank you for caring," she says. "No one else cares."

I try to smile at her. "I hope you're wrong."

"I'm not."

I leave as quickly as I can.

She's right, of course. She would know that Belrose is dead. Especially because I am willing to bet that she did it.

I blink away tears. Why can't they figure out what she did to him? Why can't the police understand that she murdered him? Why is it just me who can see it?

When I pull into my driveway, I realize that my parents are home . . . and so is Rob.

Rob Samuels.

Who is waiting in the kitchen with my parents, talking to them about God knows what, and my parents are just standing there, smiling, like I should be happy that he just showed up and is smothering me and won't leave me alone for a goddamn second.

"Look who's here!" my mom says, looking over the brim of her wineglass as she leans against the kitchen counter. My dad waves.

"Hi," I say.

Rob stands immediately. "Hey, Ri! Surprise!" He loops an arm around my shoulders right there in front of my parents, claiming me.

SUCH A GOOD GIRL

We're an *us.*

We're an item.

We're serious enough to show affection in front of my parents.

I feel sick.

He leans in and kisses me on the top of my head. "You okay?" he whispers in my ear, because he always notices things like that.

Why does he have to notice everything?

I shake my head.

No.

I'm not okay.

"Mm-hmm."

We leave my parents in the kitchen and go to my room, and Rob puts his hands on my hips and draws me into a hug. "What's wrong?"

I stare out the open window. The sun is setting on the street, and everything is falling into shadow.

"Just stressed," I whisper.

"I can make it okay," he says. "If you'd let me."

I want to tell him that stopping by unannounced is not okay. I want to tell him that being buddy-buddy with my mom and dad without my permission isn't all right, and moving in on Neta to get closer to me is really not going to work for me.

But I need him. And so I will make this work. So I let him hug me, and all I can think is that I don't fit right under his chin. Not like with Alex.

I feel strange and cold and for some reason, I feel like there's someone else out there. Someone else in the room. Someone watching.

"Can I kiss you?"

I tilt my chin up to let him, and then as he moves his face toward mine, I duck away.

"Do you want our first kiss to be when I'm this upset?" I say, burying my face against the blue cable-knit of his sweater.

"You're right, baby. We should wait."

He holds me tighter, and I feel like I'm dying in his arms. I didn't ever tell him he could call me that. I didn't tell him he could touch me. I shouldn't be in his arms. This isn't right.

My eyes flick back to the window.

"You're a good person, Rob," I whisper.

Maybe it's even true, but I don't mean it at all.

Things to Know About Riley Stone:

- In preschool, Riley actually got in trouble for kissing too many boys in the schoolyard. Her teacher threatened to use rubber cement on her lips. Of course, Riley does not count any of these as real kisses because they were (a) embarrassing and (b) in preschool.
- After Riley kissed boys in the schoolyard, she would push them. Hard. But she never actually got in trouble for pushing boys because the boys she kissed never wanted to admit they'd been hurt by a girl. Riley, of course, used their sexism to her advantage.
- Riley quit modeling at age fifteen when she won runner-up at the local modeling show she'd won every year since she was four. That year, a new judge, a Miss Brown, rated Riley low in every category.
- Kolbie won first place.
- After Riley quit modeling, she joined the Keep First Street Alive historical site fund-raiser, which was scheduled for the same date every year. The year Riley joined, the fund-raiser rented the modeling contest venue, and the annual modeling event was subsequently canceled. By that time, however, Kolbie was already signed to an agency in New York and did not see the cancellation as a slight.

THIRTY-FIVE
Car

As it turns out, a lot of geniuses were insomniacs. Groucho Marx, Vincent van Gogh, Thomas Edison—I'm in good company.

It's something about smart people, I think, being unable to turn their minds off.

Never mind that it's become a more serious problem recently, since Alex's disappearance. Never mind that I know every single little divot and crack in my ceiling, and how if I think too much about everything it all drives me a little bit crazy. Maybe I should take a Benadryl. The pharmacist told my mother to take Benadryl on any overseas flights instead of sleep aids.

My phone pings.

I roll over to answer it, pulling my already tangled sheets with me.

It's a new e-mail.

A new e-mail from Alex.

My heart almost explodes into a million pieces. He's alive. Alex Belrose is alive.

Unless it's someone else using his e-mail.

I click into the account, and there it is, plain as day: an e-mail from him to me. I can feel it. It's really him.

Meet me at the cliffs near Porter Lane at midnight.

He wants to see me. He wants to see me at the cliffs near Porter Lane.

Of course. It makes perfect sense. Everyone knows the cliffs near Porter Lane. Three years ago, it's where Paul Billson, the local mortician, got drunk and ran off the road. He almost ran straight off those very cliffs, but the fencing along the side saved him. The next morning, the police found him asleep in his car, one wheel dangling over the edge of the cliffs, about to plunge three hundred feet down into a river.

The fencing, damaged from Billson's accident, was removed and not replaced. The locals, spooked by the story, avoid the place completely.

Which is probably why Alex wants me to meet him there.

I check the time.

It's 11:46. I have to hurry.

Quickly, I pull on a hoodie, a pair of jeans, and sneakers, then slide open my window. I climb over the sill and push off, jumping clean of my mother's flowers that grow along the sides of the house, then I slip back between the flowers to quietly pull my win-

SUCH A GOOD GIRL

dow down. If I leave it open, the heat will kick on more often than normal, which might wake my parents.

I put my car in reverse and roll it out of the driveway without starting it, and then, once I'm in the street, I turn the key and pull away.

No lights go on in the rearview mirror.

I let out my breath, which fogs up the windshield. The night air is frigid. It's a bitter cold that settles deep into the bones of the earth on still nights, nights when birds and other animals tuck themselves away into nests and holes. The wind isn't blowing, not even a breeze, and the silence, even more than the temperature, makes me shiver.

I turn the heat on high and click on the radio, but for a moment, there is only static, and then a tinny old blues station comes in, like my car can't receive anything else. Then it clears up and the pop station comes through, blasting Taylor Swift too loud.

I turn it down, my skin prickling oddly.

Something is wrong. Something *feels* wrong.

But of course it does. It's the middle of the night and I've just snuck out of the house to meet my missing (and possibly presumed dead) teacher.

I reach the edge of town and turn onto the web of dirt roads that will lead me to Porter Lane. I hear the gravel crunch under my wheels even with the music on, hear it hit the undercarriage of my car as I draw closer.

I'm going to see Alex.

I'm finally going to see him.

263

The blood in my veins turns hot.

I turn onto Porter Lane, and my headlights fall upon someone: a tall figure, standing alone on the corner, in the tall weeds that the frost has been too stubborn to completely kill.

Alex.

I hit my brakes hard, my car jerking to a stop, and there he is, after so long, he's just there, looking like he's always looked, not hurt or lost or anything. I leap out of my car, leaving it running, the headlights on, and then I stop short, just standing in front of him, looking up at him, and it's him and he's there and it's just us after so long and he's okay.

"Alex," I whisper. His name, after so many days of uncertainty, feels good in my mouth. He gathers me up in his arms and kisses me, hard and long, my body against his, and it feels so, so good, like all the worry and pain from the past two weeks are just falling away, like they were never there in the first place, and I'm actually happy, just happy. He's okay. Alex is okay. I'm okay. He's back. Jacqueline didn't kill him.

"What happened?" I ask in his ear, and I realize I'm shaking. My body feels strange and tight and sore.

He pulls away, and the moonlight casts his soft features into strange, sharp places and valleys that I never saw before. "We're going to be together," he whispers, his voice a deep, long scratch. "We're finally going to get to be together."

My pulse quickens. "How, Alex? How is it going to be okay?"

"Do you trust me?" he asks.

No. The answer is in my heart, automatic and unbidden, but I

SUCH A GOOD GIRL

squeeze his hand, and then he's kissing me again, and oh my God I have missed him and for just a second I feel like my life is back together but nothing is together and this isn't right.

I pull back for a moment, my head down but my hands still on his arms and his on my waist.

"Run away with me," he pleads. "Come on. Let's run away from here. We can start over and be together. And when you turn eighteen, we can get married. We can have a family. We can forget this whole stupid town and all of these horrible people and it can be just us, forever."

I stare at him. Is this what Alex thinks I want? Babies and a family? To miss out on everything I worked so hard for? To just give everything up for him? What was the point of all the secrecy if I was so ready to throw everything away? Doesn't he realize I want to go to college? To reap the rewards I've earned for myself? That I deserve?

Doesn't he know me at all?

I step back, away from him.

I stare at the man standing in front of me, holding his hands out, pleading.

"Alex, I can't. I've worked too hard for everything here. I can't just walk out on all of my responsibilities."

"I worked for my life, and look where I am—with a wife who cheats on me and leaves me for extended periods of time? With someone who loves her stupid wine club more than she loves me? In a job that doesn't pay me enough to cover my house and car payments? I can't live like this anymore, Riley. Please. Come with me. I'm begging you. I love you. God, I love you."

265

"I love you too, Alex. But *no*."

But then he's pulling me. Pulling me away from my car that's still idling, the door open and the headlights on. "Just let me show you something," he whispers. "Let me show you how it will all be better for us. Let me show you how I keep my promises."

"Can I turn my car off?" I ask.

He shakes his head. "It won't take long. I swear. And then we can leave here."

I cast a look back at my car, but I follow him, away from the light of the car, where there's only moonlight.

"Where are you taking me?" I ask.

"You'll understand when you see," he promises me, walking faster. He takes my hand and pulls me after him, and the cold is seeping through my jeans and into my bones. What is he doing? Where has he been all this time? Is he insane?

He's smiling. He's smiling so big, like there's something I'm missing, and I've been missing it this whole time and he's waiting to draw back the curtain and show me, but it's all off, and I shouldn't be here and I know it. But I don't want to leave him. Not when I've finally found him.

"What's going on, Alex?" I try to sound calm. I'm excited he's okay. I am. But I have a feeling that's like a vibration in my chest, and it's crawling up to the back of my neck. I feel like I'm watching a horror movie, and I want to scream at the girl on the screen to stop, to turn away, to just, for the love of God, not look around the corner.

But I don't.

SUCH A GOOD GIRL

He touches my shoulder. "I have a surprise for you, Riley," he says. "That's where I've been, you know."

"Where?" My voice is casual. This is just like any other conversation we've ever had, of course. Like we're talking about lasagna or cookies or poetry or how I won't give myself to him.

I feel mad inside, like there's something inside of me screaming.

"I've been planning."

"Planning?" My voice has a funny pitch to it.

"Just wait."

He speeds up, and I match his steps. The ground beneath our feet is hard and dry, and the cold air is full of dust. The earth has been begging for moisture, but it hasn't rained in weeks—just drizzled pitifully for a few minutes one day last week before giving up.

"There," Alex says.

And at first, I don't see anything. But then a shape emerges in the darkness, large and hulking, the moonlight glinting off the glass of the windows. It's a car, black, with rust around the wheel wells—and as we get closer, I see that it's moving. Just slightly.

Rocking in the darkness, at the very edge of the cliffs.

Alex turns to me and grins. He reaches into his pocket and pulls out a small Maglite. He clicks it on before handing it to me.

"I told you it would be worth it."

"What?" I ask.

But I'm scared of the answer.

"Come on," Alex says, and we walk toward the car together. I look back at my car, which is still waiting, the headlights two beacons in the night, the door ajar.

267

And at the black car. It's still moving, ever so slightly, in the darkness.

As I get closer, I realize why.

There are people in it.

People rocking back and forth.

But—why?

"Alex—"

He holds up a finger. "Wait," he says.

We reach the car, and he opens the door grandly. It creaks, loudly, and the familiar chemical scent of gasoline reaches my nose.

Alex takes the Maglite from me and shines it inside, and there they are, blinking against the bright light and struggling against thick knots of blond rope:

Jacqueline Belrose and Rob Samuels.

Jacqueline sits in the passenger seat. Her ropes have been knotted through the steering wheel. She's been gagged and a bloody purple bruise maps across her forehead, and she's making small noises behind her gag. Noises like she's trying to scream.

Rob is looking at me, throwing his head back and forth like a wild animal, his eyes wide and lolling. He's already in some sort of pain. Alex has hurt him badly, and I can't tell how. I can't see bruises or blood, but something's wrong. Something's really wrong.

I have to get them both out of here.

Jacqueline, perhaps, wasn't the crazy one. Maybe it was Alex all along.

SUCH A GOOD GIRL

He couldn't just be patient. He couldn't just do all of this the right way. He had to go psycho and put everyone in the car at the edge of a ravine.

I feel strange and ill. But I can't throw up. I can't. I have to be calm.

"What? Alex, what is this? What are you doing?"

"You wanted me to get a divorce, didn't you? So we could be together?" He laughs. "You know Jacqueline would never leave me alone. She would have bled me dry just for her designer clothes and her stupid wine. But if she's dead, she won't be able to." He laughs again, and it's short and mad.

"And you don't think blowing her up in a car is a little suspicious?" I ask faintly. "That doesn't look like murder at all, does it?"

"I'll be gone. They already think I'm dead, don't they?"

"And what did Rob do to you?" I ask. Given, he's not exactly my favorite person, and yeah, he's been really touchy and awful in ways I haven't appreciated lately, but blowing him up in a car?

Alex's face darkens. He looks strange and unfamiliar. "I saw you two together."

And that's enough.

"It wasn't really anything. I was just trying to make sure no one knew anything, you know? About us? Please, Alex. This is a little rash, don't you think?"

I pause and grab on to the sleeve of his jacket. "You don't need to kill them, Alex."

Alex blinks at me, his eyes closing. "I know I don't." He reaches into his pocket and tosses me a book of matches. "We do. Together."

269

I take the matches and pull one off. "So you want me to help you kill them? Is that it?"

He nods, his green eyes looking almost black in the deep of the night. "That's it. This is what binds us together. Not our blood." He touches his heart. "Theirs."

I turn the matches in my fingers, trying not to look at the way Rob is still thrashing in the car, at the way Jacqueline has her head strained toward me, her bulging eyes screaming all the things she can't. I think of all the times I wished Jacqueline dead. I think of all the times I actually started planning it.

And here it is, laid out before me, in one very messy car.

My hands start to shake from fear and pain and cold.

He's insane. Alex Belrose, my first and only love, is absolutely insane. There's no way around it.

"I'll get rid of Jacqueline forever if we can get rid of Rob, too," Alex pleads. He still has that smile on his mouth, and it's twitching and odd. Something about him has gone off.

And I'm in way too deep.

"About that . . . ," I say.

And I throw the matches off the edge of the cliff, into the water below.

"You're insane!" I say. "And I have the pictures on my phone to prove it. And I'll tell everyone you tried to fail me just so you could bring my parents in to threaten me. If you kill them, I'll show everyone just how goddamned nuts you are, Alex Belrose. You let them go and you don't come near me or them again."

He crosses his arms, and the flashlight lights up his face from

SUCH A GOOD GIRL

below his chin. "P-pictures? What are you talking about? I didn't ask your parents to come in, either. And I don't know why you're attacking me like this." Very slowly, he starts unbuttoning his shirt, revealing a thin red line about his heart. "I can't lie to you, Riley. We're blood-bonded, remember? And they can test for that sort of thing now. They'll bring us in to the police station together, and they'll be able to tell we're part of each other, won't they?"

I'm breathing hard, and my heart is in my throat and my stomach and my head and everywhere all at once. I pull my phone out of my jacket and open the folder. "You snuck into my *bedroom*," I say, and my hand trembles.

He is quiet for a moment as he takes the phone, and he looks through the photos one by one.

I sneer at him. "You've gotten so good at lying you don't even realize when you do it to yourself. Do you remember now?"

He screams, then, and it's primal and animalistic, and he throws the phone down and starts toward the car.

"You did it!" he screams at Rob. "You were stalking her! She's mine! And you were after her, all this time! Fuck *you!*"

And before I can move or scream or stop him, he pulls another book of matches out of his pocket.

He lights them all at once, across the rusty side of the car.

And then he throws them in the door and slams it shut.

I grab my phone off the ground and run away as fast as I can.

I turn back, grabbing my ears, and the car is in flames, and Alex is just standing there, watching it, watching them burn, watching them die, and then it happens.

271

The explosion.

A giant orange fireball, bright as the sun, like a thousand guns going off at once, and I cover my ears and hit the ground.

But it doesn't stop me from seeing.

Alex, getting blown back by the force of the blast.

Toward the cliff.

Over the edge.

And gone.

Alex Belrose, presumed dead.

Things to Know About Riley Stone:

- When Riley Stone recounted her account of the events leading up to the murders to the police officers, her lawyer, and the DA, they were shocked that anyone could survive such a horrific incident with such grace.
- It was concluded, after an investigation, that Riley had been manipulated into a highly inappropriate relationship with her French teacher based on the threat of bad grades (and the promise of better ones).
- The photos on Riley's phone were found to have backups stored on Alex Belrose's e-mail account.
- Riley's grades had indeed been changed after the meeting with her parents, Ms. Felcher, and Mr. Belrose.
- DNA evidence from the Belrose residence corroborated Riley's story that she had, indeed, spent a significant amount of time at the Belrose residence.
- Throughout the process, Riley's bravery and fortitude were commended.
- When Riley Stone cried, the entire station cried, including the DA—who swore she hadn't shed a tear in ten years.
- The police station never knew that Rob Samuels, not Kamea Myers, had been Riley's real competition for valedictorian. He had been signed up for a special course that would have allowed him to significantly raise his GPA.

AMANDA K. MORGAN

- Jacqueline Belrose had been a successful model since she was a teen. She had once been signed with a modeling agency in Paris, which was how she met Alex Belrose while he was studying abroad.
- Jacqueline's maiden name was Brown.
- Riley has a tripod in her closet specifically made to hold a smartphone. She bought it at the mall, on clearance. She uses it to make YouTube videos, or to take timed photographs of herself throughout the night.
- Riley knows the password to Alex's e-mail account, which connects neatly to his Outlook calendar and his cell phone. It's an all-access pass to everything Belrose.

THIRTY-SIX
After

I sit at my vanity, putting the final touches on my makeup while I wait for Sandeep to pick me up.

He's been so sweet through all of this, really. So supportive. So *perfect*. I couldn't ask for a better boyfriend. Tonight will be our fourth date, and I think I'll ask if he wants to make it official. Make Riley and Sandeep an *us*.

At first I wasn't sure if Sandeep would be into dating me again, especially after what happened last time we went out, but when he found out that Alex Belrose had manipulated me against my will and tried to ruin my life . . . he understood. And how could he not? *Any* good guy would understand.

I finish my mascara and blink at myself in the mirror. There's nothing there to show that a few weeks prior, I was a girl being mentally held hostage by an insane, delusional man who believed I really loved him. Nothing to show that I was helpless. Nothing to show that I was about to watch three people *die*.

Or that I was about to take a tour of several nationally syndicated talk shows to speak about my experience. Or that soon, I was going to be on the cover of *Clare* for their "Teens Who Rock" issue. They're calling me brave. They're calling me a *heroine*. And I understand why.

Anyone else would have broken under that kind of pressure. That kind of stress.

But not me.

I made it out alive. I made it out valedictorian. And it'll probably take me some time to heal, which is perfectly understandable, but I'll be okay.

Fighters always are.

Naturally, I had to figure some details out creatively to connect the dots, but it wasn't like it mattered. Alex didn't make it off the cliff and I did, and I needed, after all this, to be perfect, just like I always had been, in order to be okay. And if Alex loved me like he said he really did, he would have understood that.

I lean forward and touch the tiny red line below my eye, where a bit of metal hit me when the car exploded. I wince. It still hurts. It will leave a small scar. But it's nothing compared to what Alex did to me. Nothing.

It's too bad about the scar. And too bad so many people had to die. But so much good has come of all of it for me. I'm rising.

SUCH A GOOD GIRL

There is a knock at my door, and my father opens it, very slowly, as if he doesn't want to startle me. "Sweetie?" he asks.

"Yes?" I smile at him in the mirror.

"Your date is here." His voice is soft. That's how they talk to me now. They pay attention when I enter the room. They make sure I get enough to eat. They smile at me, albeit a bit sadly, when they think I'm not looking.

"Thanks, Dad. I'll be right down."

"I'll let him know."

Dad closes the door.

I tie a dark pink ribbon in my hair and then uncap a tube of lipstick.

I won't put on too much, of course.

After all, I am a good girl.

Something to Know About Riley Stone:

- Riley Elizabeth Stone is just about perfect. Ask anyone.

ACKNOWLEDGMENTS

Any author knows that the hardest part of the book is often the acknowledgments—there are so many important people to thank when it comes to creating a story!

First, to Michael Strother and Jennifer Ung: Michael, you are a fantastic editor who shared the vision for this book from day one, and that means the world to me! I had a blast creating it with you! Jennifer, I am so grateful to you for adopting this book and for helping to make it the best it could be. I cannot tell you how much I value your passion and commitment to this story.

To Melissa Edwards: thank you for being so amazing and supportive. I am lucky to have you as my agent!

To my parents, for always being there, for encouraging me, and for helping me every step of the way—thank you. I love you!

To Bethany and Suz, for being amazing, always. I couldn't do it without you.

To the musers—thank you for being there for me, especially this year.

To Tammy Gibson, my early reader—I appreciate it so much!

To Teresa Kirchner, for all of the incredible advice on cheerleading—you went above and beyond for me!

To Amy Ross, Carrie Straub, and Aldo Wilson: thank you for helping out with my French!

ABOUT THE AUTHOR

AMANDA K. MORGAN is the author of *Secrets, Lies, and Scandals* and *Such a Good Girl*. Originally from Nebraska, she now lives in Nashville, Tennessee, where she is hard at work on her next novel.